MW01493962

Drummer

Dan Bomkamp

Lovstad Publishing
www.Lovstadpublishing.com

Copyright © 2016 Dan Bomkamp
All rights reserved. No part of this book
may be reproduced or transmitted
by any means without written
permission from the author.

DRUMMER

ISBN: 0692658602
ISBN-13: 978-0692658604

Printed in the United States of America

Cover photo of Civil War Re-enactment by Dan Bomkamp
Cover design by Lovstad Publishing

DEDICATION

This book is dedicated to my Dad, Mike
and my Mom, Elaine.
I hope I have made them proud.

Thanks

Without Sandy Stiemke this book would have never been written. I met her some years ago at a book signing and she told me about the Sixth Wisconsin Light Artillery and that it would make a good story for one of my books. At the time I had several books that I was working on and nothing happened with the idea. Then a few years later we met again and the more she told me about the research she'd done, the more I knew this was something I wanted to write about. So without her this book would not have happened. Thanks Sandy.

I also want to thank the Lone Rock Historical Group for their help and encouragement. They have a very nice little museum in the library and it was amazing to see things from the Sixth, including Captain Dillon's uniform coat. They were a huge help in the making of this book.

I heard a teenager on the radio talking about camp life as he participated in reenactments when I was starting to work on this book. I managed to contact him and he spent an afternoon with me answering my questions about the war and the men and boys who participated. I'd never met a kid that young who knew so much about the civil war. So I want to thank Keegan Campbell for all the great information and also for playing my character Eli for the cover photo. How nice it is to see someone so young with such a passion for something like this. Thanks Keegan.

And I have to thank my longtime friend and publisher Joel Lovstad. We met many years ago and have spent countless hours together. His advice is always appreciated and I am happy to have his friendship. Thanks Joel.

Drummer

Foreword

The American Civil War was fought from 1861 to 1865. It began with seven southern slave states declaring their independence. Eventually eleven states seceded and formed the Confederate States. The first battle took place at Fort Sumpter on April 12, 1861. After that initial battle, the war expanded throughout the southern and western states.

The war produced over one million casualties, including dead and wounded; 620,000 of these deaths were soldiers and two thirds of those were from disease. 50,000 civilians also died.

Eight percent of all white males between the ages of 13 and 43 died in the war. An estimated 60,000 men lost limbs, and 56,000 died in prison camps.

All of the major heavy industry was located in the north; the south had little industry and was mainly a farming economy. When the war broke out, most in the north thought it would be over in a matter of months. But that proved wrong and it took until General Robert E. Lee surrendered to General Ulysses S. Grant at Appomattox Court House in Virginia on April 9, 1865 for the war to end.

President Lincoln was assassinated because of feelings of those who were against freeing the slaves, but the Union was preserved.

Chapter 1

Winter 1861

My little sister died the day after my fourteenth birthday. I don't think anyone but me even remembered it was my birthday. There had been no birthday cake or celebration because my sister was so sick that Mamma didn't leave her side. It was a cold, dark February day. My Mamma wailed and cried when she died, and so did the rest of the family. She was only six years old.

Sally had been sick for about two weeks. She'd been visiting a school friend one weekend and a few days later she began feeling sick. She had a fever and soon the spots began showing. My Mamma and Dad knew right away what it was. They moved Sally to the back of the cabin and hung some sheets from the ceiling around her bed. They told my brother Jeremiah and me to stay away from her.

Jer and I didn't know what was going on but a few days before Sally died we overheard Mamma and Dad talking behind the sheets. We heard Dad say it was smallpox.

Jer motioned for me to walk outside with him. He was very sad and very afraid. I'd never seen my big brother so upset. He was seventeen and a big strong guy that I looked up to. We'd always been close and he often took me with him when he met his friends and treated me really nicely.

"We've been exposed Eli."

"Will we catch it?"

"I don't know. I hope not."

"Sally will be okay, won't she?"

Jer shrugged his shoulders. I could tell by his voice that he didn't think she would be okay.

"I don't know a lot about it, but from what I've heard, it's pretty bad. I've heard that if you get it, you usually die. Once in a while someone has some kind of immunity to it and lives, but it's a very bad disease."

"You mean she really could die?"

"She might," he said.

A few days later Sally was dead. The poor little thing suffered and cried and it was all Jeremiah and I could do to stay clear of her. We wanted to do what we could to make her more comfortable but Mamma didn't want us near her in the hope we wouldn't get sick. Sally and I had always been very close. Now, Mamma wouldn't even let me get close enough to her to say goodbye. I sat and watched from across the cabin as Mamma wrapped Sally in a blanket and then sewed the blanket around her.

Mamma came over by me and told me to get Jer and that we should dig a grave for Sally. I tried to hug Mamma but she told me to stay back.

"I don't want you to get the sickness Eli. It's best that you just keep away until we see if anyone else gets sick."

Jer and I boiled pails of water and carried them out into the back yard near the woods to thaw the ground so we could dig a grave for her.

We did all of the work and we didn't talk much. We poured hot water on the frozen ground and let it thaw and then dug the mud out. Then we boiled more water and took another layer of mud out of the ground. It took us two days. When we had the hole deep enough Jer and Dad carried Sally out and laid her in the ground. Mamma knelt by the grave and said a prayer. We all cried. Jer and I said we'd fill the hole. We could see that our Dad was not well. He started looking sickly and Mamma held him as they walked slowly back to the house.

"Dad looks sick," I said.

Jer nodded.

"Do you think he's got it?"

"He might Eli. We might all end up getting it."

"You mean we all might die?"

"I've heard of whole families that have died and even whole towns where everyone died."

Dad took to bed a day later and Mamma tried to keep him comfortable. She wouldn't allow Jer or me near him.

Dad died a little over a week later. By the time Dad died, Mamma was sick and covered with the smallpox spots. It took Mamma two more weeks to die. Jer and I buried them all. The place where I'd grown up with so much happiness was now like a tomb. Jer and I figured that one of us would be next, so there wasn't much else we could do except sit in the cabin and wait for death to come to us.

That night I lay in my bed wondering what was going to happen next. If smallpox was what Jer had said, it was only a matter of time before he or I got it. Tears came to my eyes as I thought of how lonely it was without Mom and Dad and Sally.

I heard something like a choking sound and looked over toward Jer's bed. I listened carefully and I realized he was crying.

Jer was my big brother and as tough as anyone I knew. I'd never seen him cry before.

"Jer?"

He turned his face away from me.

"Jer are you okay?"

He didn't say anything for a bit and then he turned toward me.

"No I'm not okay Eli. I'm scared to death. We've been exposed to smallpox."

"Maybe we're that immune thing."

"Pray that we are Eli. Pray hard."

We both lay back on our beds. My eyes filled with tears as I thought of how terrible it was for the ones who had died. It scared me half to death to think of it.

"God, please take care of me and Jer," I whispered.

Word spread among the neighbors and no one would come near our cabin. Finally one day about a week after Mamma died, one of Jer's friends stopped but stayed away from the cabin. He stood in the yard and we talked to him from the front door. He wanted to see how Jer and I were doing. He wanted to come up and talk with us but Jer made him stay back.

"We're not sick but that doesn't mean we won't be," he said.

His friend Leonidas said he'd take his chances but Jer wouldn't hear of it.

"If you come close you might take the sickness back and kill your whole family," Jer said.

"Can I bring you anything? What can I do to help, Jer?" Leonidas asked.

"Just pray for us," Jer said.

A week passed and we both were still feeling well. It was still cold outside so we spent most of the time in the cabin except when we went out and chopped wood for the fire. We ate almost all of the food in the cabin and were planning on going out to try to shoot a rabbit or grouse so we'd have some fresh food.

"I think we made it," Jer said one morning.

"What are we going to do? We have no money. How will we live?" I asked.

"I'm old enough to get a job. I'm sixteen now. I'll support you Eli," he said. "I've had enough schooling, so I'll find work and we'll get by."

Although I'd lost most of my family in the last month, I felt pretty happy, knowing Jer and I were going to be okay.

The next day Jer had a fever. I saw the look of dread on his face, as he got more and more sick. I decided to do what I could to keep him comfortable and take my chances that I'd not get the sickness.

"Eli, you have to stay away from me," he warned.

"Jer, I've been exposed. That's already happened, so I'm going to take care of you."

I watched my last family member get sicker and sicker. The bumps came on his body and he suffered horribly. I held his hand and fell asleep in a chair that I'd drug next to his bed. When I woke the next morning I was still holding his hand. It was stone cold. Jeremiah died during the night.

I sat there and looked at my last family member. Tears ran down my face and I knew I was next. It was only a matter of time and I'd be dead too.

I drug his body across the frozen ground on a blanket, and wrapped him in it while I dug his grave. It took me over an hour to drag him out there. He died just a week and a day after he got the fever. I'd spent hours boiling water, had the hole thawed and dug by the end of the day. I was getting pretty good at digging in frozen ground.

When I had Jer buried, I didn't know for sure what to do. The neighbors knew what had been happening and they stayed away, knowing that if they came to help, they'd be taking the disease back to their own homes and risking their lives as well as the lives of their families, so I knew no one was coming to help me.

I longed for someone to talk to and for someone to tell me that it would be okay. I wondered how it would feel to die. I wondered how long it would take before I started getting sick.

I couldn't go to the neighbors for help, so I decided to sit in our cabin and wait to die. I was exhausted by the time I got Jer buried so I lit a candle and sat alone in the empty cabin. My heart was broken and I expected to get sick soon and join my family in heaven. I fell asleep by the fireplace.

I woke the next morning and the cabin was cold. The fire in the kitchen stove was nearly out and the fireplace was completely out. I got up and stirred the embers and put some small pieces of wood into it and soon it caught fire. I put more wood into the stove and lit a fire in the fireplace, and looked around.

I wasn't used to being alone in the one-room cabin. I'd grown up with my family near me day and night. It was very quiet and lonely. I was used to having someone to talk to and now there was nobody.

My stomach hurt and my head ached.

"The fever is starting," I thought. "It won't be long now."

I thought about my friends at school and how I'd miss them. I wondered if they'd miss me. Then I thought about Franklin. I thought I should try to get word to someone to come and take care of him when I died.

Then I decided that I should get things ready for when I died, so I decided to dig my grave so when someone found my body they wouldn't have to do all that work. I had nothing else to do and it would pass the time, so I got some water from the well and filled two pails and sat them on the stove.

My belly hurt very badly. I knew I'd finally caught the smallpox. My head ached and I had chills. It was just a matter of time. I started shaking. I was terrified of dying alone in the cabin. Then deep down in my belly there came a loud growling sound. I realized I hadn't eaten in over two days.

"Well I might as well eat because when I get sick I won't feel like eating anymore," I thought.

I looked in the kitchen and found a half a loaf of bread but it was all moldy. Mamma had a little cupboard in the corner where she kept her home-canned goods so I looked there.

I found jars of beef and deer and a couple full of chicken. There were carrots and peas and beans too. I took a jar of beef and opened it and poured it into a pan and set it on the stove. Soon the smell made my belly growl again.

"Maybe the reason my belly hurts is that I'm just hungry," I thought.

When the beef was hot I got a fork and ate it from the pan. I didn't see any reason to use a plate or bowl. I ate half of the jar and felt a lot better. My headache went away too.

The water was steaming on the stove. I stood there thinking about it and decided I'd wait to make sure I was going to die before I dug another hole. I'd dug too dang many holes in the last couple of weeks and didn't want to waste one if I wasn't going to die.

Since I had two pails of hot water I decided to take a bath. It had been a while, what with all the sick people and digging holes, and I needed one. I put our big tub next to the stove and poured the hot water into it. Then I got another pail of cold water and put it in. I tested it with my hand and it was just right.

I took off my grubby clothes and grabbed the soap. I stepped into the tub and sat down. I began by washing my hair and then washed the rest of me. It seemed strange to be sitting in the middle of the cabin naked but there was no one to offend with my nudity.

When I was clean I got out and dried off. I put on some clean clothes and carried the water out and dumped it. Then I put the pails and the tub away.

I felt a lot better. I was full and clean. Now all I had to do was wait to see how long it took for me to get the smallpox.

Chapter 2

I waited two weeks and I still wasn't sick. The weather had turned warmer and I was about out of food. I was lonely and just had to get out of the cabin and do something.

All the while my family was dying, my job was to take care of our horse, Franklin. We had a small shed for him to get in out of the cold and in part of the shed was a pile of hay that we'd put up in the fall. Each day I'd go and feed and water him. He was the only contact I had all that while with another living critter.

I knew Mamma had a little money hidden under her mattress for emergencies. I found the little purse and counted the coins and found it held three dollars and ten cents. I guessed that Mamma would consider me dying of starvation an emergency, so I took the money, put on my work boots and started walking toward town.

I thought about trying to ride Franklin into town, but he was used to being harnessed up to pull our wagon, so I decided to walk.

We lived back in a hollow about two miles east of Lone Rock. There was a road that ran all the way to Madison coming from the east and it ran through Lone Rock and then on to Richland City. I walked down our lane and then along the road and went to the local general store.

I walked up on the front porch and was about to open the

door when Mrs. Sanderson, the wife of the owner stopped me. She was in the store and held the door closed.

"I'm sorry Elijah, but I can't let you in," she said from behind the door. "We've heard about your family contracting the smallpox. We can't take a chance of you bringing it in here."

"My family is all gone Ma-am. I'm all that's left."

My eyes filled with tears and I wiped them on my sleeve.

I could see her soften. But her fear of the disease kept her from letting me in.

"Mamma, let him in," I heard someone say.

"Kathy Jane, we can't. His family has the smallpox."

I saw one of the girls from my school beside Mrs. Sanderson. It was her daughter. She went to my school.

Kathy Jane was a year behind me at school. She was pretty skinny and kind of a pest but we always got along okay. I wasn't too interested in girls yet but that didn't keep Kathy Jane from following me around and asking me to do things with her. She wanted me to push her on the swing and I did that. Every so often she'd bring some cookies wrapped in a little towel and give them to me. That was okay too, but then she wanted me to take her fishing and I put a stop to that idea. Fishing was a boy's activity.

"Eli, are you sick?"

"Nope. My brother Jeremiah was the last to die. He died two weeks ago yesterday. I don't think I'm gonna die," I said.

She turned to her mother.

"He doesn't have it."

"We can't take the chance dear," her mom said.

"Can we sell him something and put it out for him?"

Her mother thought about it and then decided my money was okay.

"What do you want Eli?"

"I was hoping to get some bread. Mamma always baked

our bread but I don't know how to do it. I was hoping you had a loaf that you'd sell. I'd like some eggs too and maybe bacon. I'm not much of a cook but I think I can cook that stuff."

"Anything else?"

"Would you happen to have some cheese?"

"We have all of that. We'll get it ready, please step back off the porch."

I stepped back and stood in the path leading up to the store. A while later Kathy Jane opened the door. She was carrying a cloth sack with the groceries in it.

"Kathy Jane, you stay back," her mother said from behind the door.

Kathy carried the sack down the steps and set it on the ground a little way from me.

"Mamma is scared of you Eli," she said quietly. "I'm not though."

"Thanks Kathy," I said. "How much do I owe you for the stuff?"

"Mamma said its forty cents."

Then she whispered.

"I put in some cookies and a handful of penny candy too."

I grinned at her. She was always really friendly to me. Jeremiah teased me about her and said she fancied me. I wasn't in the market for a girlfriend. Besides she was pretty skinny and not real cute. But I was always nice to her. I tried to be nice to everybody, even girls.

I handed the money to her.

"Thanks Kathy Jane. I appreciate it."

"When you run out come back."

"I might go back and get the smallpox and die you know."

She smiled.

"You won't Eli Campbell. I know you won't."

I picked up the sack and headed back home. The sun was

shining and the snow was melting and it was a fine day all in all. As I walked along I heard someone call my name. I looked behind me and there was someone running down the road from town. I stopped and waited. After he got closer I saw it was Leonidas Honn, my brother Jer's best friend. Jer always called him Bruce since he didn't like the name Leonidas very well.

Once I asked Leonidas how he got such a strange name. He told me he was named after a Greek who was the king of Sparta, named King Leonidas who fought at a place called Thermopylae in 480 BC. He and his soldiers were outnumbered by thousands of Persian soldiers. They were known as the 300. They stood their ground bravely and were all killed. Leonidas said his name meant he'd be a brave warrior someday.

He was out of breath when he caught up to me.

"Eli, I just talked to Kathy Jane in town. She told me Jeremiah is dead."

I nodded.

"He died a few weeks ago Leonidas. Right after the rest of my family died."

His eyes filled with tears. He turned away. I could tell he was crying and didn't want me to see. A bit later he wiped his eyes and he turned back to me.

"I can't believe it. How can that be?"

"It was smallpox Leonidas," I said.

"But how is it that you're not dead too?"

"I don't know. Everyone else got sick. I didn't. It's been a long time now, so I don't think I'm going to get it."

"Well, I'm glad for that Eli. I can't believe Jer is dead. He didn't look sick when I was there a while ago."

"He started getting sick right after that."

He shook his head.

"I should have come back sooner to see if I could help," he

said.

"If you had you'd probably have the smallpox now and so would your family."

"I just talked to him a while ago about the possibility of war. We talked about signing up to fight. We thought it would be a grand adventure to go off to war together."

"What war? Who are we going to have a war with?"

"You haven't heard?" he asked.

"No, Jer didn't tell me anything about war."

"I think it's coming Eli. I think it's coming soon."

Chapter 3

Leonidas walked with me to our cabin. When we got there he walked over by Jer's grave and knelt and said a prayer for him and the rest of my family. I invited him in and he hesitated but decided to come in anyway.

"I don't know much about smallpox but I think you have to be in contact with someone who has it," he said.

"Okay, so tell me about this war," I said.

"You know President Lincoln was elected don't you?"

"I didn't know that. We don't get much news out here. Maybe my Mamma and Dad knew but they didn't talk to me about that kind of stuff."

"Well President Lincoln was elected because he promised to abolish slavery. That riled up the states in the south and now they're threatening to secede from the Union."

"What's that mean?"

"They are going to stop being a part of the United States and form their own country."

"Can they do that?"

"They say they can. Of course the states in the north don't want that to happen. So, there's a good chance there will be a war fought to keep them from leaving."

"And you want to fight?"

"Eli, do you think it's right for people to own other people?"

"You mean Negro people?"

"Yes, I mean Negro people. In the south they buy them and sell them like they were cattle or horses."

"That doesn't seem right," I said.

"It's not right. They're people just like us. But the southerners need them to pick cotton and work their farms and they won't change and free them. President Lincoln told them they have to let them go free. They won't do that and I think pretty soon there will be a war to make them do it."

"Jer wanted to fight in a war too?"

He nodded.

"Jer thought it was wrong to own slaves. We talked about it a lot. If there is a war, I want to go and do my part to keep the Union together. Plus just think of all the places we could see and things we could do. There's a big country out there away from this river valley."

I sat for a minute to think it over. I'd never been out of the river valley in my life. I had no idea of the rest of the country or the world except what I read in my schoolbooks. The idea of leaving the only place I knew was very frightening but also very exciting.

"Are you sure you're going if it happens?"

"I've made up my mind. My friend Henry Dillon is talking with other men in the area and if things heat up, he may try to organize an artillery unit."

"He can do that?"

"He was in a war when he was young and he knows about that kind of thing. You have to know who to talk to and stuff, but yes I think he can. It depends on if the southern states decide to secede or not."

"What's artillery?"

"It's big guns, cannons. They have units in the army that just shoot those big guns at the enemy."

"I'll go since Jer can't do it."

"That's brave of you Eli. But I'm not sure how old you have to be. You might be too young."

"Will you let me know if this happens? Then I can decide

and see if I'm old enough."

He smiled at me.

"You know, you're just like Jer. You look a lot like him and act like him too. He had that same brown hair and eyes and a little sly smile like you do. I think he'd be really proud of you Eli."

He got up and hugged me. He wiped his eyes and said he had to go back to town.

"Will you be okay here alone?"

"I've been alone for two months. I've got some food now and plenty of wood. I'll be okay. But I've got to start to decide what I'm going to do. I can't just sit in this cabin for the rest of my life. I have a little money but it won't last long."

"I'll check on you again in a few days. The weather is getting nice so we can get out and find out what's happening with the south."

He said goodbye and walked down the path toward town. I watched him until he was out of sight. It had been good to have someone here to talk to and to be with.

I looked over to the edge of the woods at the four fresh graves. I walked over and stood there looking down at them.

Everyone who had been important in my life was lying in those graves. All I had other than them was the cabin and the horse and a few dollars. There was nothing to keep me here.

"If there's a war and they'll let me join up," I said out loud, "I'm going."

Chapter 4

Afew days later Leonidas knocked on the door. I was glad to see him. He rode up on his horse and wanted to know if I wanted to saddle Franklin and go for a ride. It was a beautiful spring day. The snow was melting and the sun was shining and I was very glad to have something to do besides sit in the cabin. I was about out of food again too, so I thought this would be a good chance for me to stop and get some more groceries.

"Sure, but can you help me saddle Franklin? He's too tall for me to get the saddle up on his back without standing on top of the fence and the last time I tried that I fell off and nearly broke my neck."

He laughed and together, we saddled the horse. We rode down the lane slowly enjoying the warm weather.'

"Have you heard anything more about the war Leonidas?"

"Why don't you call me Bruce? Everyone else calls me that."

"Okay, have you heard anything about the war Bruce?"

He grinned.

"You're a wise-guy just like your brother."

He hesitated and I saw a little sadness creep into his face.

"I haven't heard much lately. We should stop and see Mr. Dillon. He keeps up on all the news."

We rode along talking about how glad we were to see

winter nearly over. We took the trail down to the river and stopped on the riverbank. The ice was beginning to look dark and it wouldn't be there for much longer. Suddenly we heard a lot of honking and watched a flock of geese fly up the river. If the geese were back, it meant spring was here for sure.

"Do you fish Eli?"

"Yeah, I like to fish. Jer... Jer and I used to walk down here and fish. Do you?"

"Yeah, fishing is good. Maybe when the river opens up you and I can fish a bit."

I liked that idea. Even though Bruce was a few years older than me he treated me like an equal and I thought that was nice. I suppose it was because he and Jer were such good friends but for me it was really nice to have someone to be with and talk to.

"I'd like to stop at the general store and get a few things," I said.

"We can do that," he said.

We turned the horses around and walked them slowly into town. We tied the horses up in front of the general store. I stopped on the porch. Bruce went to the door and stopped and looked back at me.

"Aren't you going in?"

"The last time Mrs. Sanderson didn't want me inside. She said I might be carrying the smallpox bug."

"Well, obviously you're not sick. Come on, let's go in."

I followed him. I didn't mind staying outside as long as I could get some supplies but if he said I should go in, I was going in.

Mrs. Sanderson gave me a look when I came in but she didn't tell me to leave.

"So Eli, you didn't get the smallpox after all."

"No Ma-am. I guess I'm lucky."

"Well thank God for that. What can we get for you today?"

I told her what I wanted and she began gathering up the things. Kathy Jane came in from the back room and was happy to see me. She ran up to me and hugged me.

"Oh Eli I'm so glad you're back and not sick. I prayed every day for you."

"Well thanks for that. I guess God didn't want me yet."

She fussed over me and told me how good I looked for all I'd been through. She even brushed my hair back and commented on how long it was getting, but how nice it looked. Bruce was standing a little way off and he was grinning at how I got flustered with her fussing so much. I knew my face was bright red.

My groceries came to fifty cents and I paid for them. Kathy Jane snuck a few penny candies into the bag as she handed it to me.

"Come back anytime Eli," she said.

"Boy that girl is sweet on you," Bruce said, grinning as we walked outside.

"She's always been like that. I don't want to be rude but I don't have much time for girls. You know what I mean?"

Bruce grinned.

"You're fourteen. Wait a few years. She'll look better and you'll like her."

I thought he was silly, but I didn't say anything. Just then we heard a loud voice from down the street.

"Stand still! How in heaven's name do you expect me to get this right with you fidgeting around like that?"

Bruce grinned and looked at me.

"Who's that yelling?" I asked.

"He's not yelling. He just has a big voice. That's Mr. Dillon, the tailor."

We were just a short way from the tailor shop. Since it was so nice and warm, the front door was open and we could hear him inside.

Soon a lady and a young boy came out and walked toward us.

"I told you to stand still," the lady said.

"He scared me Mamma."

"Oh don't be such a baby."

Bruce looked at me.

"Let's go see if he knows any news about the war."

I was a little hesitant. Any man with a big voice like that must be quite a big scary man. I wasn't sure I wanted to meet him.

"We stopped in front of the store and a smallish man with a red chin beard and moustache stepped out and smiled at Bruce. He had dark eyes that were very intense.

"Bruce, how are you today?"

"I'm fine Henry. I want you to meet Elijah Campbell. You met his brother Jeremiah some time ago. He and I were good friends."

"Yes I remember Jeremiah. You said you and he *were* good friends? What does that mean Bruce?"

Bruce looked at me.

"He passed away Sir. My family got the smallpox and everyone died except for me."

I could see his eyes soften.

"I'm very sorry to hear that Elijah. How long ago was this?"

"They call me Eli, Sir."

"Then Eli it will be."

"My little sister died first. Then my Mamma and Dad died and then Jer died about a month ago."

"And you didn't get sick?"

"No Sir, someone said I must be im..."

"Immune, Eli. That means for some reason the disease couldn't make you sick. I've known some people who have beaten smallpox. I believe I, myself, am immune. I've been exposed but never took sick."

"I guess I'm lucky," I said.

"Your family is all gone. How do you live son?"

"I'm staying in our cabin. Mamma had a little money hidden so I can buy a little food but I don't know what I'm going to do when that runs out."

Mr. Dillon looked like he was thinking about something. He stared off in the distance for a bit and then turned to Bruce.

"So what brings you boys here?

"Have you heard more about the possibility of war Mr. Dillon?"

"That, I have boys."

Chapter 5

"I was telling Eli that you'd spoken to Jeremiah and me about it. He hadn't heard of it since he lives quite a long way from town and was alone pretty much most of the last few months."

"Things are not good. There are several states that are considering leaving the Union. They are upset that President Lincoln has decreed that slavery will be abolished. They, of course, use slaves for labor and are not happy about turning them free."

"Do you think there will be a fight if they leave?" Bruce asked.

"I see no other way to settle it. I think if they secede, there will be a war between the north and the south."

"Will you go Sir?" Bruce asked.

"That I will," Mr. Dillon said.

"I'll go with you," Bruce said.

Mr. Dillon smiled.

"Well then, if it happens, I have my first recruit."

"I'll go too," I said.

Mr. Dillon looked at me and smiled.

"How old are you Eli?"

"I'm fourteen Sir."

"I don't think they'd allow a boy that young to fight. This is war. There will be people shooting at you and trying to kill you. It's not a game son."

"But I could do something useful. I have nothing here. I don't want to keep living in that lonely cabin all by myself. I'd rather take a chance on getting shot than sit out there in the woods by myself."

Tears filled my eyes. Until now, I had been mostly alone and hadn't realized how much I missed being with other people. Now I had been with Bruce and Mr. Dillon and I knew I couldn't go back to that cabin and be alone again.

Mr. Dillon put his hand on my shoulder. His big voice softened.

"You won't be alone Eli. I want you to go with Bruce to your cabin and gather all of your things. Lock it up and come back here. I've been thinking of taking on an apprentice for a while now. We'll fix you up a cot in my tailor shop and you can work for me. If and when war comes, we'll see what happens."

"What is an apprentice Sir?"

"An apprentice is a helper that learns a trade. I myself was apprenticed to a tailor when I was twelve years old. When I was sixteen I opened my own tailor shop. You can help with the work and I'll teach you how to be a tailor. Then someday you can start your own business and make a living."

"You mean it? You'll let me work for you?"

He nodded.

"It's an honest profession and I can use the help. That is, if you want to try it."

"Oh heck yeah, Mr. Dillon. I'll do whatever you need done."

"Bruce, will you help him?"

"Of course Mr. Dillon."

My heart felt lightened. All the while I'd been out on the horse ride with Bruce I'd been thinking of how I dreaded going back to the cabin alone. I was so happy that I wrapped my arms around Mr. Dillon and hugged him. I think I surprised him. He smiled and said for Bruce and me to get going so we'd be back before dark.

Bruce had a hard time keeping up. I was hurrying Franklin as fast as I could make him go.

"Slow down Eli," he shouted from behind.

I slowed down and he caught up.

"You're pretty happy," he said.

"I've been so lonely. I didn't realize it until I was out of that cabin for a while."

"Mr. Dillon is a fine man. He had his own tailor shop and then he served in the Mexican War in an artillery battery. I think you're a lucky boy to get to learn from him."

"I must be lucky. My family all died from smallpox and I didn't. Now I'm going to help Mr. Dillon. God must be looking down on me Bruce."

"That He must," Bruce said.

We rode up to the cabin and tied the horses to the corral. We went inside and I packed the few clothes I had. I looked around and thought about what else to take. I picked up Mamma's Bible and put that on the table. Dad had a pistol and a squirrel gun so I took both of them. I looked through Jer's stuff. My heart ached thinking of him. We'd been so close and always did so many things together.

"Eli, why don't you take Jer's clothes and his shoes? You're fourteen and at your age you grow so fast. In a few months or a year you'll fit right into those clothes."

"That's a good idea," I said. "And if I learn anything about tailoring, I can make them my size."

Bruce smiled at me.

"I know you miss Jer. I do too. We'll see him again someday in heaven."

I nodded.

We packed up the stuff in a cloth sack.

"There isn't a lock on the door. We really should make so no one will come in here and take anything," Bruce said.

I thought for a minute. Then I had an idea. I went to Dad's little workbench in the corner and got a little can of black paint and a paintbrush.

"Be right back," I said.

I went out to Franklin's little shed. There was a pile of planks against the wall and I chose one and opened the paint and started painting the board. When I was finished I carried it over by the door. I put the paint away and threw the brush in the weeds. Then I got a hammer and a couple of big nails.

"Help me nail this up," I said.

We closed the door and Bruce held up one side of the plank while I nailed the other side to the doorjamb. Then I nailed the other end on Bruce's side.

We stood back and Bruce grinned at me.

"That should stop them."

I looked at the plank. I'd painted on it: SMALLPOX!

I painted a skull and crossed bones on each end for those who couldn't read.

I walked over to my family's graves. I told them where I was going and that'd I'd be careful. Then I got on Franklin and rode off down the trail, to my new life.

Chapter 6

Mr. Dillon's wagon was pulled up in front of the tailor shop. Bruce and I tied up the horses and went inside. Mr. Dillon was rearranging things.

"We'll make a spot here in the back for your cot. Then we can put a curtain across the back of the room so you have privacy. During the day when we're working we'll open the curtain and put the cot out of the way," he said.

"That will be fine," I said.

"I have four daughters at home, so it would be difficult for a boy your age to stay with us there."

"This is fine Sir," I said.

"You can eat with us and spend time there and then come here and sleep. With all those girls, you'll enjoy the peace and quiet," he said smiling.

Bruce laughed.

"Those girls are spirited," he said.

Mr. Dillon just shook his head.

"I'm the only male in the house. It is sometimes, quite a task."

We carried in my stuff. Mr. Dillon cleared out a cabinet for my clothes and the rest of the stuff. Then we took the saddle off Franklin and I led him into the back of the tailor shop and put him in a pen. Mr. Dillon parked the wagon and then unhooked his horse and put him in with Franklin.

The two horses sniffed each other and then went

galloping around the enclosure.

"It looks like they're friends already," Bruce said.

"I'm sure they'll enjoy being together. Eli it will be one of your chores to take care of them. You will feed and water them and groom them when they need it."

"I'll be glad to," I said.

Mr. Dillon took a deep breath.

"Well I think we should go over to the house and have you meet the girls."

Bruce grinned.

"Oh boy."

Mr. Dillon's house was across the street and one house down. There was a lot of laughing and chatter as we walked into the front room. His wife came and met me and was very nice. Then she called the girls and they came running down the stairs.

The oldest was Susie and she was nine. Then came Mary, who was eight and Ada who was five. Jennie was the last and she was only two. Mr. Dillon told the girls who I was and they all smiled at me and said hi. Little Jennie was very bashful.

"Dinner is ready," his wife said. We all went to the dining room and I sat where I was told to sit. I was next to Susie.

"So Eli, do you have a girlfriend?" she asked quietly.

"Um, no."

"Would you like to be my boyfriend?"

Oh boy.

Mr. Dillon cleared his throat.

"Eli is a guest and works for me Susie. He will be too busy to have a girlfriend."

I looked at him and he winked.

Boy he saved me there.

After dinner I went back to the tailor shop and put my

stuff in order. The shop was pretty small and there were piles of cloth and other things Mr. Dillon used for his work. I put things so I had a nice little space for my bed my stuff. I walked to the front window and looked out.

There were houses and other buildings all up and down the street. People walked by and some rode by on horses or in carriages. It was very different from our little cabin in the woods.

I took a chair out and sat on the front porch of the shop. It was getting close to dark when I heard my name called.

I looked and here came Kathy Jane walking down the street.

"I heard you'd moved to town Eli," she said as she walked up to the porch.

"Yeah, I'm going to be an apprentice to Mr. Dillon."

She looked at me sitting and then I realized I should be a gentleman and offer her my chair.

"Would you like to sit?"

"Why that would be lovely Eli," she said.

I got up and she sat. I stood a little way away, feeling kind of nervous.

"Will you be going back to school in the fall?" she asked.

"If there's a war, I'm going."

"Will they let you when you're so young?"

"I'm not sure. I have nothing to keep me here."

"Oh," she said. She turned her face away.

Oh crap. I'd hurt her feelings.

"Well, I mean I don't have a family any more. I have friends... like you Kathy Jane."

She turned back and smiled.

"I'm glad we're friends Eli."

I nodded.

"Well my mama said not to be out after dark. It's getting pretty dark."

"Well you should go."

"Will you walk part way with me Eli?"

Oh man.

"Sure."

We started walking down the street. Kathy Jane walked close to me. I didn't know why she was so close and then she took my hand in hers.

"Um," I said looking down at her holding my hand.

"Is it okay if I hold your hand Eli?"

"I guess. You're not going to fall down or anything are you?"

"No silly. I just wanted to hold your hand."

Oh boy.

We got to her house and she stopped.

"Thank you for walking me Eli. It was very nice."

"No problem."

She walked to the house. She opened the door and waved and went in. I turned around and headed back to the tailor shop. My hand was still a little moist where her hand had been. I looked down at it.

"Well, I guess that wasn't so bad," I said. "But I don't want her to get any ideas."

I went in the shop and locked the door. I pulled the curtain across the room and sat on my cot. I pulled off my shoes and socks and then took off my pants and shirt I lay on the cot in my under shorts and pulled my blanket up over me. I snuffed out the lamp. I lay there looking up at the ceiling. My life had changed a lot in the last couple of months and a lot of it was bad... but some was good too.

"Hello God. It's Eli. I guess you know I moved. I'm doing good. Thanks for not letting me get smallpox. And thanks for Mr. Dillon and Bruce helping me. Oh and I guess thanks for Kathy Jane too. I'll try to talk to you more from now on."

Then I closed my eyes and slept in my new place.

Chapter 7

The next morning I got up and walked over to Mr. Dillon's house for breakfast. Everyone was up and the girls were all talking. It was a lot different than the quiet time I'd spent in our cabin for the last couple of months.

When we finished Mr. Dillon and I went to the tailor shop. He began working and had me watch as he cut material and marked it. He explained what he was doing and I watched closely.

After he had all of the pieces of material cut out he started putting them together. I watched as he put the cloth on a machine he called a sewing machine. I'd never seen anything like it. Mamma always just used a needle and thread but this machine sewed things together very fast and it was quite a thing to see.

We spent the morning with me watching, as Mr. Dillon put the suit together. At noon Susie brought a basket with sandwiches and some cake to the shop and we took two chairs and sat on the front porch and ate our lunch.

"So Eli, what do you think of the tailor business so far?"

"I think it's a pretty good thing. I'm not sure I'd ever be able to do it, but I think it would be a good job. I'd rather do that than work on a farm or something like that."

"Give it time. I started at age twelve. If you work at it, you can be a tailor in a few years. That is, if we don't go to war."

"Do you think war is coming?" I asked.

"I've been in communication with Senator Wilkson at the capital in Madison. He will keep me informed. But I guess, if I were a betting man, I'd bet we're going to war."

"And you'll go?"

"I'll be the first to go. I went to war when I was sixteen. War is a terrible thing but when it's necessary, all men need to stand up and fight for their country."

"Cept if you're fourteen," I said quietly.

Mr. Dillon looked at me and smiled.

"Perhaps if war does come, we can find a way. You don't know how to play a bugle or drums do you by any chance?"

"Play music?"

"Yes, you know what a bugle is don't you?"

"Yes Sir. But I don't know how to play one. Drums neither. But I could learn. Why would you ask that?"

"Well each company has its musicians. They are usually younger boys who are under the age they are allowed to fight. When there is fighting and guns and artillery are going off it gets very loud. The officers have to have a way to communicate with the artillery batteries and they do it with different cadences on the drum or different bugle calls. The sound carries across the battlefield and the soldiers know what to do by the sound they hear from the musicians."

"Wow, I could do that."

"I think the drum would be your best bet since you're not trained in either It takes a little time to master the bugle. But that might be a way for you to participate, if you're sure you want to be in it."

"I do, I really do. Jeremiah and Bruce had planned on going if it happens and since Jer is gone, I want to take his place. How can I learn the drum playing?"

"Do you know Mr. White?"

I shook my head.

"I don't know many people in town. We didn't get to town

much."

"Tom White lives down by the river. He was a drummer in the Mexican American War some years ago. I think he might be talked into teaching you."

"Really? Oh that would be great."

"Let's get back to work and after dinner tonight we'll walk down and talk to him. He's a very nice man and I think he'd be happy to help out."

I was very excited. We worked on the suit we were making. Well, Mr. Dillon worked on it and I watched. Several times people came into the shop and talked to him about something they wanted to have sewed.

"Eli can you read and write?" he asked when the first lady came in.

"Yes sir. I can cipher numbers pretty good too."

"Take that pad of paper and get a pencil. I'll give you figures and you write them down."

I got the paper and he measured the lady in different places. He told me a number and what measurement it was. I took special care to get them all down exactly as he told me. When he was finished he looked at the numbers and smiled.

"You got them just right, and your penmanship is very good. They'll be easy to read when we start on this garment."

"I got an A in penmanship last year," I said.

"And it was well deserved."

We finished up at the shop and went to his house for dinner. I was getting to feel more comfortable in his house and the girls chattered about many things while we ate. When we were finished we took a walk down the street toward river and came to a small cabin right next to the riverbank.

There was a man sitting on a chair on the riverbank with a fishing pole stuck in a forked stick.

"There's Tom now," Mr. Dillon said.

"Hello Henry," the man said. "Come on over."

We walked across the grass and stopped next to the man. He had a gray beard and was wearing bib overalls. I must have looked pretty surprised when I walked up to him.

I looked down and he only had one leg. There was a pair of crutches on the ground next to the chair. One of his pants legs was pinned up with a couple of safety pins.

"Didn't know I was a one-legged old soldier?" he asked me.

"I um, no, Mr. Dillon didn't tell me that."

Mr. Dillon shrugged.

"I must have forgotten that."

"Run over to the house and bring a couple of chairs over," Tom said to me.

I did as he said and Mr. Dillon and I sat down on the riverbank beside him.

"Well, it happened when I was just a little older than you are son."

"My name is Eli."

"Okay Eli, well let me tell you the story."

Chapter 8

"I had just turned fourteen when the Mexicans and the United States went to war. The United States had annexed Texas and that made the Mexicans mad so they tried to take California and some other land and we got into a big fight about it.

"I had two older brothers and they were going to fight and a couple of my older friends were going too, so I wanted to go. I was too young. I should have told them I was sixteen and I'd have gotten in, but stupid me, I was truthful and they said I couldn't fight. But I said I'd do anything worthwhile and they asked me if I played drums or bugle."

I looked up at Mr. Dillon and he smiled.

"So, I said I played drums. I lied like a dang snake. Well I'll be danged, if they didn't sign me up as a drummer.

"Well we were going to go to training camp in about ten days so I went on a hunt for someone who knew how to play drums. I found an old guy who played in a band and he taught me the basics. Once I got to the army camp, their musician trainer taught me the cadences and I managed to become a drummer."

"Was it hard to learn?"

"At first I dropped the sticks more than I hit the drum with them and I got blisters on my fingers, but eventually I got it down pretty well. We went off to war. There was a bugler with us and the two of us shared a tent. We became good friends and it was quite an adventure. He taught me to play the bugle and I taught him to play the drum. It was very exciting until we got into the first big battle."

Mr. Dillon smiled at me.

"Now listen carefully Eli."

"Well my friend Preston and I were with our Captain and he was directing the fight. He gave orders to the officers and it was chaos. The guns were firing and the noise was deafening. There was smoke and men around us dropped as they were hit. Preston and I were scared to death. The other side was shooting guns at us and their artillery was shooting cannons at us.

"We saw many of our men get hit and die. But we sent orders by drum and bugle to the troops and eventually we won that battle. Then we moved onto another and another battle.

"About five months into the war Preston and I were on a hilltop with our Captain and two Lieutenants. The Captain had just given the order to fire a volley from our battery when the Mexicans fired and everything went crazy. Their gun hit one of the Lieutenants and he and his horse just kind of disappeared. There was an explosion and the Captain was blown off his horse. I felt a sharp blow to my leg and fell. I passed out I guess because when I opened my eyes again, I was in the hospital tent and the physician was looking down at me.

"I asked him what happened. He told me that our Captain, one of the Lieutenants and Preston were killed. Then he said my leg was gone."

I sat there trying to take all of that in. He was only fifteen and he lost a leg?

"Oh no," I said.

"It was tough for a while. I had a lot of pain and every day I prayed that I wouldn't get infection and die of gangrene. And eventually I healed up and lived through it. I was lucky but my friend Preston and the others weren't so lucky."

"So you came here?"

"I had a brother in this area and came and stayed with him for a while. I got used to getting around on one leg and I do this and that and make a living. I get a pension from the army too."

"So Eli, do you still want to go to war?" Mr. Dillon asked.

"Yes Sir. I know it's not a game. And I know I might get hurt or killed but I'd feel wrong staying behind."

Tom smiled at me.

"You remind me of me," he said.

"Tom, Eli has the same problem you had. He's not old enough. But I think I can get him into the musician corp. But he needs to learn to play the drum."

Tom turned to me.

"Go in the house. There is a cupboard next to the stove."

I went into the house. I opened the cupboard and there behind some pots and pans sat a drum. Next to it there was a bugle lying on the shelf. On top of the drum was a pair of drumsticks. I dug them out and carried them out to the riverbank.

Tom took the drum and tapped on it with a stick. He turned some little silver buckles and tuned it up.

"Well, are you ready for your first lesson?"

"Yes Sir," I said.

Chapter 9

Mr. Dillon said he was going home to his family and that I should be at his house for breakfast at seven thirty in the morning.

I adjusted the strap for the drum and hung it over my shoulder. He showed me how to hold the drumsticks and then he took them and showed me how to make a steady beat. I tried it and at first I wasn't very good at it but he kept helping me and in a bit I had a nice steady rhythm.

"What you have to do is be consistent, and keep the beat. When your unit marches, they'll be marching to the beat of your drum. It will be how they keep in step. If you speed up and slow down, everything will go bad.

I understood and he had me hammer out a steady beat for a while. Then he showed me an added beat that added some flair. I had a heck of a time with that for a while but eventually I got it.

My fingers were getting sore and it was getting dark and the mosquitoes were coming out in flocks.

"You take that drum home and practice that new beat. Come tomorrow after dinner and we'll go from there," Tom said.

He had me hand him his crutches and got to his one foot. I walked with him to the house. I thanked him and walked up the street to the tailor shop. I went inside and lit the lamp and sat on my bed and practiced the drum.

I played for an hour or so and had it down pretty well. Tom called what I was doing, a cadence.

"So, I know a cadence," I said to myself. I was pretty pleased as I put the drum on the floor, and took off my shoes and socks. I took off my pants and shirt and got into my bed.

I shut down the lamp and lay in the dark little shop looking at the walls. It was a lot different than back in our cabin but at least I had a place to live and meals. I decided I was pretty lucky after all.

The next morning I was eating breakfast with the Dillon's. Mr. Dillon asked me about the drum lessons and I said I was doing okay at it. He seemed pleased.

We went to the shop and began working on the suit he was making. He showed me how to do many things and the suit began to look like a suit. Mr. Dillon showed me how to measure where the buttons would be and then to measure the other side of the coat for where the buttonholes would be. Then he sewed one button on as I watched.

"Can you do that?"

"I can try," I said.

"Give it a try Eli."

I positioned the button and it took me a long time, but I managed to get it sewed to the jacket. Mr. Dillon looked it over and said it was okay. Then he had me put the rest of the buttons on.

"Henry," I heard someone say and looked up.

Bruce was in the doorway smiling.

"It looks like you have a good helper," he said.

"He's learning Bruce," Mr. Dillon said.

"Morning Eli," Bruce said to me.

"Hey Bruce."

"Have you heard?" Bruce asked.

"Heard what?"

"Virginia and Arkansas have joined the seven Confederate states," Bruce said.

"That's not good," Mr. Dillon said.

"They say Tennessee and North Carolina are on the verge of going too," Bruce added.

"If that happens we'll surely go to war," Mr. Dillon said gravely.

"They won't back down will they?" Bruce asked.

"I doubt it but they still have the chance to change their minds. If they'd think about it they'd see that the north has all of the major manufacturing in the country. Most of the gun makers are in the north, and so is the heavy industry. In the south they are mostly farmers. If was breaks out, they will have a hard time against the weapons and equipment of the north. But they don't seem to be thinking about that. This makes eleven states if those last two join. We'll know in a short time if there will be war or not."

"What can we do now?" Bruce asked.

"I have to talk to Senator Wilkins and see what he suggests. You should talk to your friends and neighbors and tell them there is a good chance of war and that if it happens, we will show our support by organizing an artillery battery here in Lone Rock."

"I know many who will come," Bruce said.

"Pass the word. Tell them to be ready."

Bruce looked at me.

"What about Eli?" he asked.

"I'll see what I can do about him becoming a musician for the company. When I was in Bragg's battery in the Mexican American War, we had drummers and buglers and a fife player. I think it's very possible he can go along."

"I'm learning the drum," I piped up.

I got my drum and showed Bruce. I picked up the sticks

and played the cadence I was learning.

Bruce grinned at me.

"Well, I'm sure of one thing."

"What's that?"

"I'm sure glad I live quite a way from here. That would drive me crazy if I had to listen to it."

He ruffled my hair.

"Tomorrow is Sunday. Want to go fishing?"

I looked at Mr. Dillon.

"We don't work on Sunday. I see no reason why you can't go fishing." Then he added. "After church."

I looked at him.

"Church?"

"Unless you want my wife to preach to you."

"How about we go after noon Bruce?"

"I'll stop by. I have everything we need."

Bruce said goodbye and we went back to work. I looked out the window and watched him striding across the yard. He was tall and skinny and very confident. He reminded me a lot of my brother.

"He's a heck of a good guy," I thought to myself. I was sure glad I had him for a friend.

Chapter 10

I went to church with Mr. Dillon and his family. Afterward we had lunch and I was told to be back for dinner at six o'clock. I went to the tailor shop and took off my Sunday clothes and put on an old pair of trousers and an old shirt that had belonged to Jer when he was younger. He'd cut the sleeves off it and I thought it made a good fishing shirt. I didn't bother putting on shoes since we were going to fish.

Bruce showed up and he was dressed in fishing clothes too, but he had on shoes. He was carrying a little wooden box with fishing stuff in it. He also had two fishing poles in his hand that he'd cut from a grove of willows.

We took off walking toward the river.

"So how is it going working for Mr. Dillon?" he asked.

"I like it. I have a place to sleep and good food, and I'm learning a trade."

"He's a good man."

"You like him a lot don't you?" I asked.

"I admire him. He's a hero you know. He went to war when he was just a kid and fought bravely. I hope to be like him."

"You will Bruce. I'm sure you will."

We got to the river and Bruce took me to his secret spot. There were a lot of tracks in the sandy riverbank, so I thought it might not be too secret. He had a little tin can full of worms so we baited up our hooks and swung our lines out into the water. We sat back against two trees a little way apart. Bruce took off his shirt and shoes.

I looked at him sitting there. He had a lot of muscles, like my brother had. I was still pretty skinny. I wished I'd get more muscles like he had.

"What are you thinking about Eli?" he asked.

"I was just thinking I'm pretty skinny compared to you."

He laughed.

"You'll grow. Don't worry."

Just then Bruce's pole began dancing and he grabbed it and pulled. He fought the fish for a bit and then pulled in a nice catfish. He took it off the hook and put it on a string through its gill and mouth. Then he put it in the river and tied the string to a bush.

"Your turn," he said.

We fished for a couple of hours and he caught three more and I caught two.

"Mr. Dillon is going to the State Capital this week to talk to Senator Wilkins about getting an artillery company organized," Bruce said.

"Really? He told you that?"

He nodded.

"I'm going with him. I want to be a part of all of this. The sooner we get started the sooner we'll be ready to go if war comes."

"You think it's coming don't you?"

He nodded.

"There are nine states now that have seceded. North Carolina and Tennessee are going to join up too and when that happens, it'll start."

"It's scary but it's exciting too," I said.

"I think you have a good chance of going along if you learn that drum."

"I hope I can. I'd hate be stay behind with the women and children."

"You'd have the pick of all the girls," Bruce said grinning.

"I'm not in the market for a girlfriend," I said. My face felt hot.

"That Kathy Jane is sweet in you Eli," he said.

"Oh jeez Bruce."

He laughed.

We fished for another hour and caught several more catfish.

"Come on, let's go back to town and clean these fish. You don't want to be late for dinner."

When we got back we stopped at Mr. Dillon's to show him our catch. We'd ended up with fourteen nice catfish.

"We could have a fish fry," Mr. Dillon said.

"We'll clean them."

Bruce and I cleaned the fish while Mr. Dillon's wife made the rest of the food for a fish fry. Bruce stayed for dinner and we had a wonderful meal.

"Do you want to go along Tuesday?" Mr. Dillon asked me.

"To the capital?"

He nodded.

"Could I?"

"Bruce is coming. You might as well come too."

"What about the shop?"

"We'll put a note on the door. I'm the only tailor in town. They'll come back if they want something."

"That'd be great. I've never been to the capital"

Bruce walked with me to the shop and said goodnight.

"I'll see you Tuesday Eli," he said.

"Thanks for taking me fishing Bruce," I said.

"It was fun. Jer and I used to fish a lot. I'm glad to have a new fishing partner."

I put my arms around him and hugged him. He didn't pull away and he hugged me back.

"Thanks again," I said.

Chapter 11

On Monday we were busy in the shop. I was now the button man. Mr. Dillon said I did a good job on buttons and buttonholes, so from now on that was one of my jobs.

When the day was over, I went down to see Tom. I played the cadence he'd taught me and he said I was doing very well. He taught me another cadence and I played a while and then went back to the shop.

It was a nice evening so I took a chair out on the porch and sat down. There were people strolling up and down the street. I was daydreaming when I heard my name being called. I turned and looked and here came Kathy Jane.

"Eli, I'm so glad I found you home," she said.

"Hello Kathy Jane," I answered.

She held out a plate with a little towel over it. I took the plate and lifted the towel and there was a pile of cookies on it.

"I made those just for you," she said blushing.

"Wow, thanks."

I took a cookie and had a big bite. It was really good. She stood there watching me.

"Oh sorry," I said. I stood up and offered her my chair.

"You're such a gentleman Eli," she said as she sat down.

I sat on the floor of the porch. I was still wearing my

fishing shirt and barefoot.

"Were you at the river?" she asked.

"Yes, Bruce and I went fishing."

"Oh how exciting. Did you catch anything?"

"We caught fourteen catfish."

"Oh my. You must be a very good fisherman. I went fishing once a long time ago. I really had a good time. But no one in my family likes to fish, so I don't get to go."

Oh boy. If that wasn't an opening, I'd never seen one.

"Oh, that's too bad. Bruce had all of the fishing tackle. He let me use his stuff. I don't have any of my own."

"We have fishing items at the store. I bet Mama would let me take a few things if I told her we'd bring home some catfish."

Uh-oh.

"Well um, that might be okay, but I really am getting a lot of work here. Plus I'm taking drum lessons from Mr. White. So I don't have a lot of time."

"Drum lessons?"

"Yes, he's teaching me how to play the drum, so if there's a war, I can go along and be the drummer for the unit."

"You're going to war Eli?"

"Well if there's a war, I'm hoping to go."

She looked upset.

"What if you get hurt Eli? Mr. White lost his leg. He wasn't much older than you are."

"I want to do my part Kathy Jane. I'd feel awful if all the other guys in the area go and fight for our country and I stay home with the women."

She stood there a second and then she put her arms around my neck and hugged me.

"You're so brave Eli. If you go I'll pray for you every day."

I was a little flustered. I'd never been hugged by a girl before so it kind of took me by surprise.

"Well um, that would be good," I said.

We stood there for a minute. I wasn't sure what to do next.

"Well I should be getting home," she said.

"Thanks for the cookies Kathy Jane," I said.

"You're welcome Eli."

She hesitated and then I'll be darned if she didn't hug me again. Then she hurried down the street.

I watched her go. That was really something getting hugged like that. I wasn't sure I liked it but I wasn't sure I didn't like it too.

I thought of how soft her hair felt against my cheek.

"Well," I said, "she makes pretty good cookies too."

Chapter 12

r. Dillon, Bruce and I got on the train Monday afternoon as it made its return trip to Madison. We each had a little carpetbag with some clothes in it. Mr. Dillon told me to take some clean clothes so I'd be presentable when we met the Senator. The train went through Lone Rock in the morning and on to Avoca and down the river and then late in the afternoon it came back. I'd never been on a train and it was pretty exciting for me. The countryside flashed past pretty fast.

Mr. Dillon and Bruce talked about how to go about recruiting men for the unit and I listened because I didn't know a thing about all of that stuff. We stopped at several towns and people got on and off. It was late in the afternoon when we pulled into Madison.

I was spellbound looking out the window at all the big buildings. I'd never seen such buildings. There were many people in buggies driving past on the streets and it was a very busy place. We got off the train and Bruce ran down the platform and talked to a man on a buggy. Soon he pulled up next to us.

"Where to sir?" he asked Mr. Dillon.

Mr. Dillon told him the name of a hotel and off we went. I could see a short way from the street and there was a big body of water.

"Is that the river?" I asked.

"No Eli, that's Lake Monona. On the other side of the land here, is Lake Mendota. Madison is built on an isthmus between the lakes.

"A what?"

"An isthmus. That is a narrow strip of land between two bodies of water. The capital is right in the middle of it."

"But we're not going there now?"

"No our appointment with Senator Wilkson is tomorrow. We'll stay the night and then see him in the morning."

I was pretty excited. I'd never been in a hotel so that was going to be something new for me.

We pulled up in front of a big building and Mr. Dillon paid the man with the carriage. We went into the hotel. It was very fancy. We walked up to a big counter and Mr. Dillon asked for two rooms.

"You don't mind sharing with Bruce do you Eli?"

"Oh no. That's fine with me as long as it's okay with Bruce."

"You don't snore do you Eli?" Bruce asked.

"Huh? Jeez, I don't think so. How would I know when I'm sleeping?"

Bruce and Mr. Dillon laughed and we went up to our rooms

We went into our room and put our bags down. Mr. Dillon told us to meet him in the lobby in an hour for dinner. Bruce took off his shoes and lay on the bed.

"This is pretty fancy, huh?" he said.

"I've never seen such a fancy place. Do I sleep on the floor or what?"

"We can share if you don't mind," Bruce said.

"That's fine with me."

"As long as you don't fart."

I looked at him and then he started laughing. I took off my

shoes and jumped up on the bed. It was like sleeping on a cloud. I bounced up and down and Bruce laughed.

"I think I'll take a bath," he said.

"I think I'll enjoy this big bouncy bed," I said.

He took his clothes off except for his underwear and then picked up a towel from the dresser and walked down the hall to the bathroom.

I must have dozed off because when I woke up Bruce was sitting on the edge of the bed putting his shoes on. His hair was wet, so I knew he'd come back from the bath.

"How was it?"

"Oh it was great. They have all the hot water you want."

"Do I have time for a bath?"

"I think so if you get going right away."

I hurried and took off my clothes and went to the bathroom. The bathtub was copper and was twice as big as the one we had in the cabin. There was a pipe over the edge of the tub with a handle on it. I turned the handle and hot water ran into the tub. Holy smokes.

I filled it half way up and then put in some cold water to make it just perfect. Then I got in and lay back until just my head was sticking out.

"Holy cow, this is really nice," I said to myself.

I took the soap and washed my hair and then the rest of me. When I got out I noticed a chain attached to the side of the tub. I lifted it up and it was stuck to the bottom, so I tugged on it and the water began leaving the tub.

"All the modern conveniences," I thought.

I dried and wrapped the towel around my waist. Bruce was sitting looking out the window.

"All clean?" he asked.

"That's a nice bathtub," I said.

"Pretty fancy. We better enjoy a bath now. When we get to the war, it'll probably be a long time between baths. And we won't have a big copper one with hot water if we do get one."

"You talk like it's sure that we're going."

"The news is that things are heading that way Eli."

"Then I better practice my drum."

We met Mr. Dillon and went to the dining room in the hotel. We all had steak and potatoes and apple pie. It was a wonderful meal. I'd never eaten in a hotel before so it was something I'd never forget.

Then we walked around downtown Madison for a while. We walked past the capital building.

"This is the second capital. The first one was in Belmont."

It was a big building but not what I expected.

"I thought it would be more grand." I said, "Like the hotel."

"The way the state is growing, I expect they'll build a bigger one someday. For now this one serves its purpose."

We went back to the hotel and Mr. Dillon said to meet him in the dining room at eight o'clock in the morning. Bruce and I got undressed and into bed. He shut off the lamp.

We lay there a while and I looked over. Bruce was awake.

"Bruce, what do you think about girlfriends?"

He turned to me.

"Are you thinking of having a girlfriend Eli?"

"No, heck no. But Kathy Jane, she keeps coming around and being friendly with me. I'm not sure what do to about it."

He smiled.

"I've had a couple girlfriends. They're a lot of work Eli. You have to be careful not to hurt their feelings and then if you want to go fishing or something you have to ask them if it's okay. Sometimes you want to just sit and do nothing. Then they want you to do some fool thing."

"So it's not a good thing."

"Oh I didn't say that. The good part is nice. I mean, they

like to kiss and stuff, and it can be a lot of fun."

"Kissing? How about making cookies for you?"

"She made cookies?"

I nodded.

"Oh boy Eli. She likes you a lot."

"So what do I do?"

He lay there a minute.

"You like cookies?"

"Sure, who doesn't?"

"There you go. She likes you and will make you cookies. See what happens next."

"Oh."

"Go to sleep Eli," he said.

"Okay, goodnight Bruce."

"Night Eli."

Chapter 13

We met Senator Wilkins and a man from Prairie du Sac named Clark. I didn't understand much of what they were talking about. Bruce seemed to be very interested. After a while Mr. Dillon asked me if I wanted to look around the capital and I said I did, so I walked around looking at paintings and things. Then I sat in a nice soft chair in the hallway outside the meeting room. I leaned back and in no time I fell asleep.

"Eli?"

I opened my eyes and there stood Bruce.

"What? What happened?"

"You were sleeping. Our meeting is over."

I looked and saw Mr. Dillon shaking hands with the Senator and the other man. Then he walked our way.

"So Eli, did you have a nice nap?"

"I'm sorry Mr. Dillon. I didn't mean to fall asleep."

"It's nothing. Come if we hurry we can make the train west. If we miss it we'll have to stay another night in Madison."

We hurried to the hotel and got our things and then hired a carriage to the train station. We made it with a few minutes to spare.

On the way home Mr. Dillon and Bruce talked about how to recruit men to the unit. I listened and then said I would be glad to make some bills to put up in places so people would see them. They thought that was a good idea.

"We'll make the tailor shop our headquarters. Anyone who wants to sign up can come there and do it," Mr. Dillon said.

"I'll be the first," Bruce said smiling.

"I expected nothing less," Mr. Dillon said.

"How about me?"

"For now, you will be my records keeper. When the men come in, you will take down their information and have them sign their name to a book. I expect there will be days when you will be very busy with that Eli."

"I'll do anything I can to help Sir."

The next few days were very exciting. I made some bills about volunteering for the unit and we sent them out with men from the town to other places so people would know about it.

Mr. Dillon worked on some of the tailor work that he had started but stopped taking in new work. I did what I could. I mostly sewed on buttons and made buttonholes. That was my job.

Every evening I went to see Tom and he taught me many new different cadences for the drum. I was getting the hang of it pretty well.

Then one evening he threw in something that made it more difficult.

"Eli, have you seen marching?"

"You mean when people all walk together?"

"Yes, they walk in step. Military units march."

"I think I know."

"Well show me."

Tom described how to march. He couldn't show me because he only had one leg.

I tried it. I wasn't very good at it.

"Try while I count."

I stepped off and he counted, one, two, three, four, left, right, left, right."

I managed to get it right after a while.

"Okay, now try it while playing your drum. Play the slow cadence."

I hung the drum over my shoulder. Tom told me to play once through the cadence and then step off on my left foot.

Well, when I marched, I couldn't keep the beat. Then as I got the beat back, I stopped marching. Tom laughed.

"Not so easy is it?" he said.

"Are you sure we'll do this?"

"Armies march Eli. When they are moving from place to place they march and the drummer sets the pace."

"Oh boy."

"Practice Eli, practice."

The next day Bruce and Mr. Dillon were talking about the artillery unit. I didn't have anything to do so I went down by the river and took my shoes off and marched in the sand along the riverbank. It was horrible. But I marched upriver and then back downriver. And then I marched again.

I took a break and heard someone walking in the woods. I turned and looked and it was Kathy Jane.

"What are you doing down here?" I asked.

She came out of the woods. She was carrying a basket.

"I heard you were down here marching," she said.

"Bruce!"

She giggled.

"I thought you might like a little snack."

Well I was pretty hungry. She came over and sat by me in the grass. She opened her basket and handed me a piece of apple pie. Then she got a little jar of milk out of the basket and handed it to me.

"Wow, thanks Kathy Jane," I said.

She smiled.

"So aren't you having any?" I asked.

"No I ate at home. How is the marching going Eli?"

"Not very good."

"Can I help?"

"What do you know about marching?"

"I know how it is suppose to look."

"It's harder than you think."

I finished my pie and milk. Kathy Jane begged me to show her my marching skills. I finally gave in.

I made a feeble attempt. She tried to keep a straight face but she broke out laughing.

"Let me try it with you. Maybe if I count and you drum it will help."

She pulled up her dress a little way and took off here shoes and stockings. Then we got up and she held her dress up so her feet and legs showed and we stepped off together.

"Left, right, left, right," she said.

We marched together down the riverbank. When we got to the end of the sand we stopped.

"Okay this time you play the drum. Don't watch your feet. Listen to my voice."

We marched up the bank. It wasn't perfect but I managed to play and march at the same time. When we got to the other end she was smiling widely.

"See Eli, you can do it."

I looked at her, smiling and standing there in the sand barefoot. She was not such a pest after all. In fact, I was getting to like her a bit.

We marched up and down the bank until it got dark. Then we put our shoes on and walked back into town. When we got to her house we stopped.

"Thanks Kathy Jane. I think I can do it now. Thanks to you."

"It was fun Eli."

Then she put her arms around me and hugged me. Her hair was against my cheek. It smelled nice.

"Good night Eli Campbell."

I watched her go into the house. Hmmm.

Chapter 14

M r. Dillon went to meet the train the next day when it came from Madison. He went every day to see if there was any news from Senator Wilikins about the war. I was cleaning up the shop and he walked in. His face looked very pale.

"Is something wrong?" I asked.

He handed me a letter. I took it and read?

Dear Mr. Dillon,

It is with heavy heart that I must inform you that our worst fears have been realized. The Confederate states army attacked the Union Army at Fort Sumpter on 12 April. President Lincoln declared war the next day.

It is time to start gathering troops and preparing them for the upcoming events that will change the face of our country forever. All of the things we discussed as possibilities are now realities.

I ask you to start gathering your men and training them. We are readying Racine as a training and preparation point for all artillery units before their deployment to the south.

Please keep me apprised of your implementation and readiness.

Yours in the name of the United States,

James Wilkins, Senator

I looked up at Mr. Dillon.

"So it's started," I said.

"I'm afraid it has," he said. "Now we have to put forth all of our efforts to recruit a unit and get them ready for war."

My insides felt strange. It was a feeling of being a little frightened, but it was also a feeling of being excited. Even though I wasn't going to be able to carry a gun and fight, I was going to do my part.

"What do we do first?" I asked.

He smiled at me.

"You're sure Eli?"

"Mr. Dillon, if I stayed behind with the women, I'd never forgive myself. I have to go."

"You saw what happened to Tom."

I thought of Tom with one leg.

"Yes Sir. I'm willing to take the chance."

He put his hand on my shoulder.

"You're a brave young man Eli."

"So, what's first?"

"Take your horse and ride out to Bruce's house. Tell him and then you and he can start spreading the word. We'll send out posters to the surrounding towns and set up the tailor shop as the recruiting station and hope that many men come in the next few days and weeks."

I rode Franklin bareback. I'd been riding him more lately and he was accepting it better. I'd only fallen off a couple of times in the last few weeks.

Bruce was splitting firewood when I rode up.

"Hey, a helper," he said.

"The war's started!"

"What? How do you know?"

I told him of the letter. He listened intently.

"So we need to tell some people and have them tell more. Then put up posters and get the unit going," I said.

Bruce grabbed his shirt. He ran to the house and told his mom what was going on and we headed off.

"We'll go over to Samuel's. He can get word to a bunch of people up that way and then we'll go over to Thomas' and do the same."

We rode all day. My butt hurt like heck by the time we got back to Bruce's house.

"I'll make up some posters tonight and we can take them around to Richland City and other places," I said.

"Okay, I'll hitch up our buggy. It'll be easier than riding bareback for you."

I grinned.

"My butt is pretty sore. But I didn't fall off once," I said.

"You're quite a man Eli," Bruce said.

"What time will you come over to pick me up?"

"How about eight o'clock? I have some chores to do first thing in the morning."

I said I'd be ready. I rode toward town. I looked back and Bruce was putting the horse in the corral. I had to smile watching him. He reminded me of my brother so much. I was really glad I had him to kind of take Jer's place.

When I got back Mr. Dillon was working in the tailor shop. He'd moved some things so that we had a small table in the front that we could use to sign up men to enlist in the unit. I told him of our plans to take posters the next day and he thought it was a great idea.

We went home for dinner and then I went right back to the tailor shop and started lettering the posters.

I was working on them when I heard a footstep on the porch. I looked up and Kathy Jane was looking in the window.

"Hi Kathy Jane," I said.

"What are you doing Eli?" she asked as she saw the pile of posters.

"The south attacked one of the forts that the northern soldiers were holding. The north declared war. Mr. Dillon got word today to get the artillery unit organized. I'm making posters so Bruce and I can put them up to get the word out."

She looked distressed

"How old do you have to be to fight Eli?"

"Sixteen," I said.

She looked relieved.

"But I'm going. That's why I learned to play the drum. I'll be the drummer."

"But you won't be where you might be hurt will you?"

"Tom White was a drummer Kathy."

Tears filled her eyes. She put her arms around me and hugged me. I was a little flustered and tipped my chair over.

"I um Kathy Jane," I stammered.

She let loose of me.

"I'm sorry for being so forward Eli. I'm just very worried that you might get hurt or worse."

"That's very nice of you to worry about me Kathy Jane. I promise I'll be really careful."

The lamp flickered and I looked at her standing there in the dark shop. She looked different than she used to look. Her hair was all brushed out and lay over her shoulders. It looked very light blond too.

"You don't wear pigtails any more?"

"Eli, I'm fourteen now. Pigtails are for little girls."

"You're fourteen?"

"Same as you Eli."

"When was your birthday?"

"Last week."

"I'm sorry I didn't know about it. I would have gotten you a present."

She smiled.

"That's sweet Eli. You don't have to buy me anything. I'd just like to spend some time with you. That would be the best present you could give me."

"Oh um. What kind of time?"

"Take me fishing Eli."

"Huh? You're a girl. Girls don't fish."

"Eli Campbell! Why would you think that girls don't fish?"

"Well, you get dirty when you fish and you have to touch worms."

"I can bait my own hook, and I'm not afraid of a little mud."

Holy smokes. I didn't know girls fished.

"Well, okay then."

"Okay what Eli?"

"I'll take you fishing for your birthday."

She broke out in a big smile and put her arms around me and hugged me again.

"Oh thank you Eli. How about Sunday after church?"

"Okay, yeah, I can do that."

She squeezed me hard. And then she kissed me on the cheek! She turned and ran out of the shop.

I stood there wondering what had just happened. Holy smokes. Kathy Jane fished and she kissed me. I stumbled over the chair I'd tipped over and fell on my butt.

I sat there and touched my cheek where she'd kissed me.

I smiled.

Chapter 15

Bruce and I left the next morning with a roll of posters and a hammer and some tacks. We went to Richland City and then to Richland Center and all of the little towns in the area. While we were nailing up the posters we often were asked about the war and Bruce explained what Mr. Dillon was doing.

By late afternoon we were nearly home.

"Well, I think we did a good job today Eli," Bruce said.

"We put up a lot of those posters. Now if only men will come to sign up."

"They will. The pay will get a lot of them to sign up. Thirteen dollars a month is pretty good wages for many of these men. They'll get uniforms and food all the while they're in the unit too, so that will be something that will change many of their minds."

It all sounded very exciting to me. I'd never been anywhere and this was a chance to see a lot of the country.

"Does a drummer get paid?"

"I think so Eli. They can't expect a drummer or bugler to do it for nothing."

"Wow, thirteen dollars. I've never had that much money in all of my life."

Bruce grinned at me.

"You could settle down and get married Eli."

I looked at him grinning.

"Why would you say that?"

"I've seen how Kathy Jane looks at you Eli. That girl likes you a lot."

"Well we're just friends. I'm not looking to get married."

"But you might be someday," Bruce said.

My face felt really hot.

"Jeez Bruce," I said.

He laughed loudly as we rode along.

Mr. Dillon sent posters on the train to other towns and he was excited about getting started on the unit. We worked in the shop to get everything finished so when the time came, he would be ready to go off to the war.

I went to Tom's house every evening and he taught me different drum cadences and I actually got pretty good at drumming and marching.

"Has Dillon found a bugler yet?" Tom asked me.

"Do we need a bugler too?"

"Yes the bugler plays different bugle calls to tell the unit when to fire the guns and when to do many things."

"I suppose we'll have to find one," I said.

"A unit really needs a fife player too. They play when you march."

"Holy cow, we'll have more musicians than soldiers," I said grinning.

Tom laughed.

When I walked out of the church Sunday morning Kathy Jane walked up to me and was smiling.

"What time will we be leaving Eli?"

"Oh you still want to go fishing?"

"Eli Campbell, you promised."

"I'll take you fishing. I have to dig some worms first."

"I have a can of worms. I dug them yesterday," she said.

"You dug worms?"

"Eli!"

"Jeez, well I'll go change clothes and come by the store and pick you up," I said.

Bruce walked over by me and was grinning like a fox.

"Do you want to borrow my fishing poles Eli?"

I looked at him. He thought this was very funny.

"She dug worms," I said.

Bruce laughed all the way to his house. Then I got the fishing gear and headed back to the shop. I put on a pair of old bib overalls that I'd cut off at the knees, and a shirt that I'd cut the sleeves off. Then I got my lucky straw fishing hat and walked to the store. Kathy Jane was waiting on the porch.

She was wearing a light blue dress and was barefoot like me. She had a can full of dirt and grass, and I guessed, worms. She also had a picnic basket.

I carried the basket and the poles and we walked to the river. She talked all the way.

When we got to the river we picked a spot and then baited up the hooks. She baited her own hook.

I watched her and she looked at me.

"What? You didn't think I'd bait my own?"

"I don't guess I did. I never saw a girl who fished before."

"Well Eli, I might surprise you."

We fished and sat in the sun and soon we were talking about all kinds of things and having a real good time. Kathy Jane laughed and was really fun to be with. She caught the first fish and then I caught one. Then after a while we washed our hands in the river and she opened the picnic basket.

"I brought some chicken and biscuits," she said.

Holy smokes. The chicken was really good, and the biscuits were the best I'd ever eaten.

"Did your Ma make these?" I asked.

"Eli Campbell... I'll have you know I made the chicken and the biscuits."

"Wow you're a good cook."

"Why thank you Eli."

Dang, she looked nice sitting there on the riverbank. I'd never thought of her as pretty but for some reason she really looked nice right then. She saw me looking at her.

"What's wrong Eli?"

"Huh? Oh nothing. I was just thinking."

She blushed.

"Will you miss me when you're off fighting?" she asked.

I nodded. "Yeah, I will."

"I'll miss you too Eli. I'll think of you every day and I'll write."

I nodded.

I had a feeling in my belly that I'd never felt before. Dang, I really was going to miss her. I was going to miss her... a lot.

We fished for a while and caught more fish. When we were done we had seven fish. She told me to take them home and the Dillon family could have them for a fish fry. We gathered up the stuff and walked back to town. On the way she took my hand in hers.

I looked down at her holding my hand.

"Is that alright Eli?"

I grinned at her. "Yeah."

When we got to the store she sat the picnic basket on the steps. She came up to me.

"I had a wonderful time Eli. I'll never forget it."

"I had a nice time too Kathy Jane."

She looked to see if her mother was in the window. She wasn't. She stepped up to me and put her hands on my shoulders and leaned forward and kissed me... right on the lips.

Then she ran up and picked up the basket and into the store.

I stood there kind of dazed. Holy smokes. I turned and started walking down the street. Dang.

Chapter 16

The first recruits showed up on Monday afternoon. Mr. Dillon and I were in the tailor shop and two men walked up. One was about Mr. Dillon's age and the other was younger. They were father and son.

They talked with Mr. Dillon about the unit and said they were ready to sign up for it. Mr. Dillon was very happy to get his first recruits. Bruce had signed up as soon as we got the proper papers so we already had one member of the unit. Mr. Dillon got the papers he'd obtained from the Senator and I sat next to him and watched as he filled in the men's names and where they were from, their ages and occupations and birth dates. Then he asked them to sign next to their names. Both signed. We had our first two members, after Bruce's name. We were up to three men.

When they left Mr. Dillon was very happy. We were still talking about it when a man walked up who was from Bear Valley. He also wanted to sign up. Mr. Dillon had me do the paperwork and watched that I did it right. That man couldn't write his name so he made an X next to where he should have signed.

The rest of the day, men and young men, not much more than boys came in one at a time or sometimes by the twos or threes. We had seventeen recruits by evening.

Many of the men who came in the next week were farmers, but there were others who were needed for special jobs. One of the early men who signed up was a preacher from Richland Center who would serve as Chaplin. We had another who said he was a cook in a hotel. One after another our unit was taking shape.

About two weeks into it three young guys came in from Bear Valley. They were all brothers. Their last name was Crary. The oldest was Martin who was twenty, and then there was Milton who was seventeen and last was Oscar who was fourteen.

I called Mr. Dillon over to the table where I was signing them up. I told him the ages. He told them that the older two were welcome but Oscar was too young and couldn't sign up. The young one was very upset about it. His eyes filled with tears and he ran outside.

I looked at Mr. Dillon and said I wanted to talk to the kid. He took over and I walked out and found him sitting by a big tree in back of the shop. I walked over and sat down by him.

"That's not fair!" he said.

"Yeah, I know," I said.

"How old are you?" he asked.

"I'm fourteen too."

"Are you going?"

I nodded.

"How?"

"I'm the drummer. Musicians can be younger. They can't fight or carry a gun but they have their duties too."

"Really? How many drummers do they need?"

"There's one drummer for each unit. But... they need a bugler."

"A bugler?"

"You don't know how to play bugle do you?"

He shook his head.

"I'd learn."

He gave me a big grin. I liked this kid. He had big friendly blue eyes and a wide smile. He was tall and thin and had black hair that hung on his forehead. He and I were about the same size and he had something about him that made me think if we got to know each other, we'd be good friends.

"Let me talk to Mr. Dillon."

I got up and went into the shop. I told Mr. Dillon about the kid and asked him about the bugler job.

"If he can learn, he can come along."

I talked to his brothers and they were fine with it. So I went out and sat down by him.

"There's a guy in town who taught me to drum. He's very talented and knows how to play bugle too. If you want to meet him, I'll take you there and we can see if you can play the bugle."

"Holy smokes, really? Oh boy, sure I'll do anything to go along. I want to be with my brothers and don't want to miss out."

I told Mr. Dillon what we were doing and Oscar and I walked down to Tom's house. Tom was sitting in the garden. We walked up and he greeted us. I saw the kid look at his missing leg.

"Tom this is Oscar. He wants to learn to play the bugle."

Tom saw him looking at his missing leg.

"I was your age when I lost that," he said.

"You were in a war?"

"Yes I was. I was in the Mexican/American war and was the drummer for an artillery unit. My best friend was Preston Andrews. He was the bugler. We shared a tent and had an exciting adventure until we were hit by artillery. Our Captain, one of the Lieutenants and Preston were killed, and I lost my leg. I'd just turned fifteen."

Oscar looked a little shaken.

"I can teach you to play the bugle Oscar, but you have to know, bullets and cannons don't know the difference between soldiers and musicians."

"I still want to go," he said.

Tom smiled.

"Brave lad."

Tom told me to go get the bugle from the house. I took it down from the shelf and carried it out and handed it to him. He held it in his hands and his eyes filled with tears. He turned away from us for a minute.

"This bugle belonged to Preston. He had his name engraved in it," Tom said.

He turned the bugle and there was the name Preston engraved in the bell on the end.

"He was like a brother to me. We shivered in our tent when it was cold and sweat when it was hot. We shared our food, our clothes and we even made plans that when the war was over we'd go off on some adventure to some exotic land."

He wiped some dust off the bugle and handed it to Oscar.

"Take care of it," he said.

"I'll treat it with all the respect it deserves," Oscar said.

"I know you will."

"But can I ask you something?"

"What is it son?"

"Call me Preston. The bugle has that name on it. I'd like to be called Preston to honor him."

Tom's eyes filled with tears. He nodded.

"I'd be honored to do that son."

We sat on the ground in the garden and he showed Preston how to buzz his lips to make the bugle play. Then he played a bugle call. It sounded pretty neat.

He handed the bugle to Preston. He put it up to his mouth and blew and it sounded like someone was murdering a cow. We laughed and laughed but Preston kept at it and after a while he began making noises that weren't as ugly.

Tom taught him how to change the pitch by how much pressure he made on the mouthpiece and told us to take the bugle and for Preston to practice. We thanked Tom and said we'd be back the next day.

"What do you think of Tom" I asked.

"I like him. He's quite a man."

"I wanted you to meet him not only for the bugle, but to see what can happen."

He nodded.

"It scared me at first. But I don't want to stay behind while all the others go off and do their duty."

"So you want me to call you Preston now?"

He grinned.

"I never liked the name Oscar anyway."

Chapter 17

P reston's brothers were in town yet and he met up with them and they headed back to Bear Valley. He said he'd be back to see me soon.

I watched them go with him sitting in the back of the buggy blowing on the bugle. His brothers weren't impressed with his music.

I told Mr. Dillon about Preston and he said if his parents were okay with him being the bugler it was okay with him.

Over the next days there was a steady stream of men and boys who came in to sign up. I kept busy writing their names and information down and Mr. Dillon talked to them about when we'd be leaving and to keep in touch so they'd be ready when we were called up.

Two days later Preston walked into the tailor shop. He was carrying the bugle.

"Mr. Dillon this is Preston and he's our bugler."

"I thought your name was Oscar."

"Nope, it's Preston."

He looked at me and winked.

Preston gave us a sample of his playing and I was pretty surprised. It didn't sound like an animal being murdered any more. We went to Tom's and Tom was impressed too.

"I'll teach you all of the calls," Tom said. "Can you come to town every day?"

"I walked here today."

"From Bear Valley?"

"Yes Sir."

"He can stay with me," I said.

"Really?" Preston asked.

"Sure, we'll figure something out."

I went back to the shop and Preston stayed with Tom to learn the bugle calls. I told Mr. Dillon that he was going to stay with me in the shop. Mr. Dillon thought it would be too crowded so he went home and got a tent he'd had from when he was in the army. We put it up in the back of the shop and I moved my cot out there. We got another cot for Preston.

I was pretty happy to have a new friend and someone to spend my free time with.

A few days later a man came in that looked familiar to me. When he spoke I realized it was Mr. Clark from Prairie du Sac. He was organizing the men up there to join up with our men to form the unit.

"How is it going here?" he asked me.

"We have a lot of men who have signed up. We have our drummer and a bugler too."

He smiled at me.

"Which are you?"

"The drummer."

"You still need a fife player."

"We haven't had anyone sign up for that."

"I know a boy who would love to go along but is too young like you. He's quite musical."

"Can he play fife?"

"I'm not sure but we have a man in the city that teaches musical instruments. I'll talk to them."

"That would be great. If he wants to go, bring him down here and he can get to know Preston and me."

"I'll do that," Mr. Clark said.

A few days later Mr. Clark drove up on a buggy with a kid sitting beside him. The kid was tall and very skinny. He had red hair, sparkling blue eyes, and lots of freckles. He had a wide grin as he climbed down from the wagon.

"Eli, this is Foster."

"Pleased to meet you," he said.

"So you play fife?" I asked.

"I make an attempt. I think I can get it with a little more practice. Maybe if the war holds off three years I'll be good at it."

I looked surprised. Mr. Clark and the kid laughed.

"Just fooling. I'm pretty good at it."

"Did you bring your stuff?"

He nodded.

"Preston is in the tent," I said pointing to the back yard. "You can bunk with us until we leave."

"That's mighty kind of you," he said.

He grinned a lopsided grin. I could see mischief in his bright blue eyes. He was going to be fun.

Over the next weeks, we signed up a lot of recruits. Bruce started coming to the shop every day to help and it got really busy. By the end of August we were approaching the number of men that we needed to become a unit.

"As soon as we get the last few recruits, you and Bruce can go to Madison and take the paperwork to the Senator and we'll get our commission as the first unit of artillery," Mr. Dillon said.

It was pretty exciting. A few days later we had our full complement of men and Mr. Dillon spent a day filling out the papers. The next afternoon Bruce and I got on the train as it was heading back to Madison. We had a leather pouch with all the papers inside it.

"In a few weeks we'll be leaving Eli."

"Leaving for war?"

"We'll have to go and have training first. Henry told me there is an artillery-training camp at Racine. We'll go there and get outfitted with our artillery pieces and guns and uniforms and then we'll go wherever they send us."

I was pretty excited as we arrived in Madison. We walked to the capital but the Senator wasn't there so we were told to come back in the morning.

"We'll have to hurry so we can make the train before it leaves," I said.

"Well if we don't see him in the morning I think we can leave the papers with his office people."

Bruce and I spent the night in the same hotel we'd been in before. We ate a nice supper and then walked around Madison.

"This is a pretty big town," I said.

"The capital was at Belmont, but they moved it here some years ago. I expect that it will become a pretty big city someday."

"Bigger than this?" I asked.

"Oh lots bigger."

We got up early and had breakfast. We went to the capital. The Senator wasn't there yet so we left the paperwork with his secretary and hurried to the train station. We wanted to get back to help Mr. Dillon get things in order.

We were getting close to becoming a real army unit.

Chapter 18

It was getting very close to the time we'd be ready to go off to war. Preston, Foster and I soon became great friends, living in our tent in the back of the shop. We ate meals with Mr. Dillon's family and then had our own place to sleep and spend time together. We went to the river and swam and fished and it was nice to have someone my age to be with. Of course Kathy Jane was my age and she came over a lot too.

Foster had a lot of fun teasing me about having a girlfriend. But when I came back from spending an evening with here with a plate of cookies, he thought it was okay after all.

In late September Mr. Dillon got a letter from the Senator and called me and asked me if I'd go and get Bruce. I found him and we went back to see Mr. Dillon.

"I got our commission as an artillery unit," he said.

"That's great," Bruce said and took the paper to look at it

"Wait, it says we're the 6th Wisconsin Artillery. We were the first ones there," I said.

"Did you give the paperwork to Senator Wilkson?"

I looked at Bruce.

"Well he wasn't there so we gave it to a secretary."

"Well something happened and it got lost and now we're not the 1st Wisconsin Artillery, we're the 6th."

"Maybe we can have it fixed," I said.

"It really doesn't make any difference," Mr. Dillon said.

I knew Bruce was disappointed and so was I. We'd worked hard to get our men and get the papers to the capital and now we weren't going to be the first after all.

Mr. Dillon told us to get the word out that we'd have a meeting to elect officers in a week, so we traveled to many of the nearby towns and put up posters.

On September 25, 1861, about 150 men assembled in Lone Rock to elect the officers of our unit. Mr. Dillon was elected Captain and Mr. Clark and Thomas Hood were elected Lieutenants. John Francher and Daniel Noyse were elected 2nd Lieutenants.

Bruce was elected a Corporal. He was very proud to be an officer even if it was the lowest officer there was. He looked at me and winked. I was pretty proud to call him my friend.

After our meeting was over we all were very excited. We were leaving on October 2 to be mustered in at Racine. Everyone had to get their lives at home settled so they could leave and know that their loved ones were going to be okay. Of course I had no loved ones so I didn't have to worry about that.

Preston and his brothers went to Bear Valley to spend time with their family and Foster went back to Prairie du Sac to say goodbye to his family. I was left alone in our tent. The work in the tailor shop was all done, so I really didn't have much to do but practice my drum.

I was banging away the next day when someone called from outside the tent.

"Who is it?"

"Eli, it's Kathy Jane."

I jumped up and pulled the flap open. I was really glad to see her.

"Come in," I said stepping aside.

She came in and looked around. The place was a little

messy with some clothes lying on my cot. I picked them up quickly.

"This is nice," she said.

"Well, it's only temporary. We're leaving in a few days."

She got a very sad look on her face.

"I hate to see you go Eli."

"I have to go. I want to do my part."

"I know, but it scares me to think you might be hurt, or... worse."

"I'll be real careful Kathy Jane."

We stood there kind of awkwardly for a minute.

"Want to take a walk down by the river?" I asked.

"That would be lovely."

We walked down the street and then when we got to the river we took off our shoes and walked in the shallow water along the riverbank. The water was warm and the sun was shining. It was a beautiful day.

"If I write to you, will you answer?" she asked me.

"You'll write?"

"Of course. I want to know what you're doing and that you're alright."

"Sure, I'll write back," I said.

She smiled at me and then she took hold of my hand. We walked along down the riverbank, holding hands.

Chapter 19

I walked Kathy Jane to her house. It was almost dark when we got there.

"Well, I better get inside. I probably missed dinner and Ma will be upset," she said.

"Sorry for making you miss your dinner."

"It's okay. It was worth it to spend such a lovely afternoon with you Eli."

My face felt hot. I didn't know for sure what to say or do.

"Well, I'll see you before you leave," she said.

"Yeah, sure."

Then she leaned forward and kissed me... right on the lips. She smiled and then she ran up the steps and into the house. I stood there for a minute. Wow! That kissing thing wasn't so bad after all.

I was walking down the street to the tent when I heard my name called. I looked and Mr. Dillon was sitting on the front porch of his house. I walked over.

"So were you fishing?"

"No Sir."

"I thought you came from the river," he said.

"Well I, um we went for a walk."

"You and Kathy Jane?"

I nodded.

I could see he had a grin on his face.

"Bruce tells me you're sweet on that girl."

"Oh that Bruce. You can't believe him."

He laughed.

"Eli, there's nothing wrong with liking a girl. One of these days you'll think she's pretty great."

I grinned.

"I already do."

He burst out laughing.

"You missed dinner."

"I'm sorry. I'll be okay until morning," I said.

"Come in, we had roast beef. I'll have one of the girls make you a sandwich."

I got a sandwich and thanked him and headed for my tent.

When I got there Preston was lying on his cot sleeping. He woke when I came in.

"I thought you went home," I said.

"I did but I want to practice some more with Tom before we leave."

"Are you learning a lot of calls?"

"Yes, I know about ten already."

"Ten? Are there that many?"

"There are more than that but many of them aren't used very much."

I sat on my cot and ate my sandwich.

"Eli?"

"Yeah."

"Do you think some of us will get killed?"

I hadn't really thought about that very much. I hoped it wouldn't happen but we were going to war.

"I hope not. But I think some will die," I said.

"Are you scared?"

"No. I think if it's my time to go, I will. I just hope it's not my time. Are you afraid?"

He shook his head.

"I'm going to do my job and hope for the best," he said.

"We'll watch out for each other," I said.

"Yeah. Hey Eli?"

"What?"

"I'm glad I have you for a friend."

I smiled at him.

"Me too Preston."

Chapter 20

The next days were very busy. Foster came back and he was anxious to get going. Everyone was getting their affairs in order so they could leave. I arranged for Franklin to stay with Captain Dillon's horses and his girls promised to be nice to him. He was all the family I had left and I hated to leave him behind.

Preston, Foster and I spent some time with Tom. He went over the calls with us and said we were ready. I think he was going to miss us seeing him so much. When we got ready to leave the last day he hugged each of us.

"You boys keep your heads down and watch your back. Don't let any of those rebels sneak up on you. Do your job and come back home when it's done."

"We will Tom," I said.

Preston hugged the old man.

"Thank you Tom. I'll take good care of your bugle."

I hugged him too.

"We'll see you in a while," I said

I looked back when we were a little way down the street. Tom was still sitting in his garden watching us. I was going to miss him.

We were leaving in the morning. Preston went home to be with his folks and family, Bruce did the same and Captain Dillon and his family were together. Foster went back to Prairie with Lieutenant Clark for one last goodbye. I didn't have anyone to be with. I sat on a chair by my tent and checked my bag to be sure I had everything in it.

I heard someone walking toward me.

"Hello Eli," Kathy Jane said.

"Hi. I'm glad you came to see me."

She came up to me and I got another chair for her.

"You're all ready to leave?"

I nodded.

She wiped her eye.

"I'll miss you Eli Campbell."

"I'll miss you too Kathy Jane."

"Will you write to me?"

"I will."

She was crying quietly. I put my arm around her shoulder and held her.

"I'll be real careful. I'm not going to be shooting or anything. So nobody will see any reason to harm me," I said.

"So how did Mr. Tom get hurt?"

"That was an accident."

"It could happen to you."

"Kathy Jane, I'm the luckiest guy in the world. My whole family died of smallpox and I lived. I'll be okay."

She handed me a box.

"I made you some cookies."

I smiled at her.

"Thank you. I'll enjoy them on the train tomorrow."

She stood up.

"Well I have to go back. Mama said I couldn't stay long."

We stood there for an awkward minute. Then I put my arms around her and she kissed me on the cheek.

"Come home to me Eli."

She turned and ran off into the darkness.

I sat a while longer and then went in and got into my bed. A thousand thoughts ran through my head.

The rush and bustle of organizing the company and the

trips to Madison and the meetings and election of officers were all very exciting. But now the idea of where we were going and what we were going to do was settling in. We were going to war. Only a couple of the whole company knew what war was like.

I closed my eyes.

"God, this is Eli. I'm sure you know we're going off to fight the war. I hope you'll keep your eye on us and help us win and help us not to get hurt. Can you tell my family that I'm safe and sound?"

Chapter 21

There were many people at Lone Rock to see us off. The train arrived and we began boarding it with our gear. There were a lot of tears from the wives and children who were staying behind. While it was exciting it was also sad.

I saw Kathy Jane standing in the crowd looking around. When she saw me she ran to me and put her arms around me. I saw Preston watching and he grinned. I knew I'd hear about it all the way to Racine.

"Goodbye Eli," she whispered into my ear. "I'll think of you every day and pray for you."

"I will too Kathy Jane. I promise I'll come back. Then we can go fishing a lot."

She smiled at me.

"So girls fishing aren't so bad?"

"Not so bad."

I leaned down and gave her a big kiss. I think I surprised her and I actually surprised myself too. When we broke the kiss she was smiling.

"Boy, you better come home," she said.

Preston hugged his Mom and Dad and he had a hard time letting go of them. His brothers finally got him to go with them to the train. Captain Dillon told me to go to the car that he and the officers were in so both Preston and I boarded that car. Foster was already aboard with Lieutenant Clark.

"You aren't going to believe what Eli just did to Kathy Jane," Preston said to Foster. They had a big time kidding me and then the train began moving.

"Well here we go," I said.

"Yeah, here we go," he said.

"Don't worry, a lot of the men say that this war will be over in a few weeks or a few months at best. They say the south can't stand up to the Union army."

"Maybe we'll be back by next summer?"

I shrugged. I had no idea.

We were coming into Madison and looked to the south side of the tracks. There was a big encampment and soldiers marching and lots of tents.

"Is that where we're going?" Preston asked.

"This is Madison. I'm sure it is. I've been here two times with Captain Dillon and Bruce. We're going to Racine."

"Well this looks like an army camp," Preston said.

I caught Bruce's eye. He walked over to our seat.

"Is this where we're going?"

"This is Camp Randall. This is Madison Eli."

"I didn't know there was another camp."

"There are many all over the country. This is an infantry camp. We're going to Camp Utley. That's an artillery camp."

"Will we just keep going on this train?"

"No we'll change trains in Madison and take one that goes to the south. We should be getting to the station soon."

It wasn't long after and we got to the station and all changed to a train that would take us to Racine.

Everyone had brought a lunch. Foster, Preston and I shared ours with each other. I showed him them box of cookies that Kathy Jane had given me.

"She fancies you Eli," Foster said grinning.

I felt my face get hot.

"You fancy her too! I can tell the way you blush," Preston said. "And that big smooch you gave her makes me sure of it."

"Shut up Preston. You talk too much."

We all laughed and laughed. Preston wasn't so dumb.

Camp Utley was pretty much like Camp Randall except that there were hundreds of artillery pieces standing in long rows. There were several artillery units there to train and it was mass confusion.

We finally were led to our area to make camp. The officers and some of the other men were taken by wagon to get supplies. When they came back Captain Dillon was fuming. The officers had a meeting and then they divided up the tents and gear as best as they could. There were not enough tents and there were only a few uniforms for us. The army hadn't gotten the stuff shipped out in time so we were going to have to make due with what we had.

Preston, Foster and I were supposed to get what they called a dog tent. They were for the lowest ranks. Every two men got one half of a dog tent. Then they buttoned them together and put pole in each end and they had a whole tent. There were no ends on the dog tents. Since the three of us were small it was decided that we all could share one tent.

Each man got a gum blanket. It was a piece of canvas with tar on one side to make it water proof. They were put on the floor to keep the men in the tent dry from the ground. They also were to be used as a poncho when it rained.

Each soldier got a half a dog tent and a gum blanket and they carried it in their backpack. At least that was the plan but there weren't enough dog tents to go around so many of the men had to sleep three to a tent.

Bruce called us over to the wagon where they were handing out the tents.

"They don't have enough of them. Since I'm an officer I get a little bigger tent like an A frame. Lt. Noyes and I are sharing a tent and we talked and would like you three to share with us. They're quite a bit larger than the little dog tent and when we get more of the little ones you guys can have your own. That way we can give your dog tent to some other men and it will help the crowding."

"Are you sure Lt. Noyes is okay with it?"

"Danny's a good guy. It was his idea."

I looked at Preston and Foster.

"Well at least we'll have ends on our tent," I said.

I'd met Lt. Noyes when he signed up. He asked about being the chaplain for the unit, since he was a young minister who served Spring Green, Prairie du Sac, and Bear Valley before the war. There was already a chaplain so he joined and was elected as a 2nd. Lieutenant. He was a very friendly young guy and I thought we were lucky to get to know him.

When all the gear was passed out Captain Dillon had Preston blow the assembly call and everyone gathered around.

"Men we've been shorted on supplies. The army has failed to get the proper amount of tents and uniforms here which is something we will soon come to realize is the 'army way'. We'll have to double up and make do. Get your selves organized and we'll have the cooks set up a mess area. Tomorrow we'll fall in and be sworn into the United States Army by Captain Trowbridge. Then we'll begin training.

"The gun units will train on loading and firing the artillery pieces. The horse units will harness and get their houses sorted out and begin training them to pull the guns. Everyone has a job and if we learn to do those jobs correctly and quickly we'll make a fine showing. We'll be ready to show the rebels what the men from the Buena Vista Artillery are made of!"

There was a loud cheer. Spirits were high. Everyone was excited. Soon we'd be decked out in our new uniforms and we'd board a train to take us to the fight. Little did we know that it would be five and a half months of snow and cold weather before we finally left Camp Utley.

Chapter 22

There was a lot of confusion and noise as officers rounded up their men and everyone found the place where they were to be quartered. The men who took care of the horses were in one area near the animals, the cooks were near the kitchen tent and the gunners were all in one area. We met Lt. Noyes and the five of us set up the tent in the area where the main officers were going to be. The Lt. explained that Preston, Foster and I needed to be near Captain Dillon and the other officers so we could send signals by drum or bugle when they wanted them sent. That made sense to us.

Our tent was twice as big as the dog tents and it had ends on it. A dog tent only had sides, so it was open on the ends. That was okay as long as it was nice weather but if it got cold those tents were going to be pretty uncomfortable. Preston, Foster and I put our gum blankets and packs in the tent and then helped some others set up the officer's tents. By late afternoon our camp was up and pretty orderly.

The cooks began building fires to cook over and soon we smelled food. Captain Dillon told Preston to blow the mess call and everyone gathered to line up for the evening meal.

Preston, Foster and I stood in line with our tin plates from our packs. When we got to the front of the line we got a big spoonful of beans with a little meat of some kind in them and a biscuit. There was a pail of water and we each took a ladle of it and put it in our tin cups. We found a place next to a tree and sat down.

"Beans," Preston said.

"You don't like beans?"

"I'm not real crazy about them but I'm pretty hungry."

We dug in with our spoons. The beans were not great but they were hot and they filled our bellies.

"I wonder what that meat is?" I asked.

"Probably one of the horses died," Preston said grinning.

"So what do you think of the army now?" I asked.

"Well so far I guess I'm not real impressed. I'm ready to get to the south and get in the fight."

"I heard some men talking a while ago at home and they think the south will be finished in a short time. They have no manufacturing in the south and there is no way they can outlast the north."

"I hope we get there in time to see some fighting," Preston said.

"Me too."

We finished up and rinsed our plates in a tub of water. Then we wandered around the camp. We went by the horses all staked out on ropes between trees. They had hay and grain and water and looked pretty content.

"I kind of miss my horse," I said.

"I kind of miss my mom and dad."

"We'll see them again soon enough," I said.

Chapter 23

Preston, Foster and I went to the tent we were going to share with Bruce and Lt. Noyes. They were already there and had their gear on the ground sorting it out. Bruce introduced Preston and Foster to Lt. Noyes.

"He's pretty old," Preston whispered to me.

"He's a little over thirty," I said.

"Yeah, old."

"When we're in camp and in our tent, you guys just call me Danny," he said.

"Me too," Bruce added.

"We should call you Danny too?"

Bruce grinned.

"When we're out with others around call us by our rank but otherwise just use our names."

We all put our gum blankets on the ground of the tent and then Danny and Bruce each took a corner. The three of us took the other side of the floor. It was a little crowded but it wasn't too bad and we were happy to have a dry place to sleep. We were glad we had a tent like this instead of the little dog tents.

Bruce had a candle that he lit and stuck in a jar so we had light.

"Captain Dillon told me to have you play reveille at six o'clock," Danny said.

Preston looked unhappy.

"You mean I have to get up so early?"

"You're in the army now," Bruce said with a grin on his face.

"I'm glad I play drum," I added.

"I'm, glad I play fife. You don't need a fife to wake people up," Foster added.

Preston looked glum.

Bruce and Danny each had a blanket and the three of us each had one too. We lay next to each other with Foster in the middle. We were all pretty skinny so it worked fine.

We all took off our shoes and hats and settled down. Bruce blew out the candle.

"Good night all," Danny said.

We all said goodnight.

I was just about asleep when I heard a loud noise. I wasn't sure what it was so I listened. Suddenly it came again. It came from my bed. It was Preston.

"What a pig," I whispered.

He giggled. Then he lifted up the blanket.

"Holy smokes!"

I fanned the stink away.

"I told you I wasn't too crazy about beans," he laughed.

"We'll have to have a firing squad in the morning," Danny said.

"Yeah, or a hanging," Bruce said.

We laughed for quite a while and then I drifted off to sleep.

I woke when Bruce got Preston up to play reveille. He yawned and groaned but he got up and put on his shoes and went out of the tent. Bruce and Danny put their shoes on and started getting ready for the day.

Preston played reveille and soon there were noises and talking all over the camp. Men started walking to the mess tent and we all walked down there together. There was coffee and oatmeal for breakfast. The guys and I sat down next to a tree and looked down at our tin plates with a big gob of oatmeal on it.

Foster looked up at me.

"What? I asked.

"Oatmeal."

"Not your favorite?"

"It would be okay if we had a little sugar or honey for it."

I took a spoonful of the stuff. It was sticky and tasted like pretty much nothing."

"We'll have to see if we can find some sugar someplace," I said.

After breakfast the officers gathered their men and went off to drill. The men who would load and fire the guns went to practice and the men who would load the guns up to be transported practiced that. The men who took care of the horses fed and watered them and everyone had a job, except Foster, Preston and me. Our time would come but right now we had nothing to do.

We walked to the mess tent and asked if there was anything we could do to help. The cooks put us to work right away.

The day passed and before we knew it we were back in our tent getting ready for bed. Danny and Bruce talked about the training.

"When do you think we'll leave for the war?" Preston asked.

"Captain Dillon said there are no travel plans for a while."

How long is a while?"

They didn't know.

The next day mail came. Everyone gathered around and some got mail and some didn't. I didn't expect anything because I had no family but my name was called. Bruce was handing out the mail and he grinned slyly at me when he handed me the letter. It was from Kathy Jane.

My face turned red.

"I'm gonna read it later," I said.

I went back by my friends and then I snuck off by myself. I opened the letter.

Dear Eli,

The word around here is that you're still training in Camp Utley. I hope you're having a grand adventure. It is very quiet here, with so few men left.

Is there anywhere there to fish? I bet you miss fishing. When you come home I hope you'll take me fishing again.

I pray for your safety every day. Be safe.

Your friend,

Kathy Jane

That first week passed and the next came and went. October was past and November was on us. The weather turned colder and the men in the dog tents were having a hard time keeping warm. We got more tents now and then and we started getting uniforms and shoes a little at a time. Preston, Foster and I got our uniforms because we were small and they had a lot of small ones. The men who needed the regular sizes were still wearing their own clothes.

The officers all got uniforms. There was some grumbling about it but there was nothing anyone could do about it.

We were surprised when we got our uniforms that the shirts were red. We'd expected them to be white. I asked Bruce why they were red.

"Artillery wears red shirts," he said. "Cavalry wears a yellow shirt and infantry wear blue shirts. It's a way of keeping track of everyone," he added.

"I like the red ones."

"Yeah they look good... but of course they stand out pretty

DRUMMER

much. We'll make good targets with such a bright colored shirt."

I must have looked strange because Bruce began laughing.

"If it's your time, I don't think the color of your shirt matters Eli," he said

We started having a lot of time with nothing to do. The men drilled and drilled and eventually they had their jobs figured out so daily drills weren't necessary. Captain Dillon told everyone they could take an afternoon and go into town and relax. The guys and I went with the group but had to stay behind when they went into some taverns.

"That's not the place for you," Bruce said.

"We'll just look around."

We walked the streets and looked into some stores. We found a mercantile store and went in. Foster and I each had two pair of socks and Preston only had one because we expected to get some from the army but never did.

We found some and they were twenty-five cents a pair.

"I don't have any money," Preston said.

"I've only got twenty five cents," Foster added.

"I have some. I'll buy us each two pair."

We got our socks and then Preston saw the sugar. We bought some sugar and some molasses.

We were pretty happy with our purchases. We walked back to camp and eventually the men started coming back. Some were pretty silly. They'd spent their time at the taverns.

The days passed and it got colder and many of the men were suffering without decent blankets and lodging. Captain Dillon tried his best to get help from the army but it seemed like the wheels moved slowly.

Then one day two old men from Lone Rock pulled up in the camp in a wagon. They had it filled with blankets and heavy clothes and tarps to make the tents warmer. Everyone was very happy with the things they'd brought.

It was good to know that our friends and relatives were there for us.

They also had a bag of mail from home. I got another letter from Kathy Jane. I read it several times and then put it with the other. I could picture her in my head with her golden hair and pretty eyes. Dang, I missed her, even though she was a girl.

Life slowed down for the next weeks and months. There wasn't much to do but wait for the army to send us to the war. We asked every time Captain Dillon was near and he always had the same answer. He'd let us know as soon as he found out.

The men were allowed to go to town pretty much any time and everyone made do through the winter months. We played a lot of checkers and cards in our tent with Danny and Bruce. I began to really like Danny.

I found that he came from Massachusetts and had gone to a college called Yale. He became a Congregational Minister and had preached at Spring Green, Mineral Point, Prairie du Sac, and had organized the First Congregational Church of East Ithaca, which was at Bear Valley. He was married and had gotten married after he enlisted in the army.

He was a correspondent for the Wisconsin State Journal and wrote stories for the newspaper. He had little to write about that winter but he expected to have many exciting tales of the war to write about and mail back to Madison when we got into the fight.

We spent many evenings talking and the five of us became very good friends.

Chapter 24

Christmas came to our camp. The married men missed their wives and families and the unmarried ones missed their girlfriends and parents. I had no one to miss. Well except Kathy Jane. Then on the day after Christmas the mail came. The men gathered near Captain Dillon's tent and one of the officers got up on a wagon and called out their names if they had a letter.

I was sitting near the tent tending our fire. There were campfires all over the encampment now. Every four or five tents had a common fire so the men could sit and warm up near it.

We had some benches we'd made out of planks and some barrels and I was sitting poking a stick into the coals when I heard my name. I looked up and Lt. Sweet was waving a letter at me.

I went up and got it and went back by the fire. I opened it and it was from Kathy Jane:

Dear Eli,

I hope this letter finds you in good health and spirits. I'm sorry to hear you're still in Wisconsin. It must be hard living in tents in this cold weather.

We are all fine here in Lone Rock. Of course we all miss our relatives and friends. We're very proud of our brave soldiers. It's quite lonely though.

I miss seeing you Eli. I miss our walks and fishing with you. I say prayers for you every night. Please be careful and stay well.

Your friend,
Kathy Jane

"From your girlfriend?"

I looked up and Bruce was standing warming his hands by the fire. He was grinning at me.

"It's from Kathy Jane. She's not my girlfriend. We're just friends."

"Sure."

That guy! He thought it was great fun to tease me about Kathy Jane.

"Have you heard anything about when we're going to the war?'

He shook his head.

"Captain Dillon and the other officers are mad as hornets. They complain every day but the army is a slow moving outfit. It looks like we'll be here for a while yet."

I shook my head. It wasn't that I wanted to get into the fight so soon but I knew it was a lot warmer in the south and I'd have liked that.

"We should get paid soon though," Bruce said.

"We didn't get paid for October or November yet," I said. He grinned.

"That's what I'm talking about."

"But it's almost the end of December."

"That's the army way Eli."

We did get paid a week later. Many of the men had charged things at the stores in Racine and by the time they paid their bills off they were nearly broke again. I had a few cents left from the money Ma left behind so I had my whole pay. I didn't know for sure what to do with it. I wanted to have some money for sweets and things but I didn't need much. I hated to keep a lot of money in my pockets.

"My brothers and I are going to send part of our pay home to our parents," Preston said to me as we carried wood for our fire.

"I don't have anyone to send it to."

"How about your girlfriend."

I turned and Bruce was standing behind us.

"She's not my girlfriend. But that is a good idea."

"Can you trust her?" Preston asked.

"I'm sure I can."

So I got an envelope and sent eight dollars to Kathy Jane and told her to hang onto it for me. I thanked her for her letters and told her I was good and hoped she was too. Then I sent it with the other mail.

Preston, Foster and I went to town and loaded up on penny candy and we each bought a pair of gloves and two pairs of socks.

January seemed like it would never end. The camp was covered with snow and there were paths from tent to tent and to the latrines and mess tent. With several men in each tent it was livable but I don't think I got really warm the whole month. We had plenty of blankets and the worst part of it was the boredom.

I got to know many of the men because there was little to do so I'd go to the mess tent and sit and watch them play cards. I noticed one man who had an accent and found out he was from Poland. His name was Milolay Dziewanoski and I never did learn to pronounce his last name. I called him Mikey.

He told me stories of how his father had been an aristocrat in Poland and when the Polish revolution happened, he lost his lands and inheritance. He decided to leave Poland and ended up in Avoca.

He was a very well liked man and contributed a lot to the village and the area. Mikey was one of the men who rowed a boat across the river to enlist in the Sixth.

He was very funny and joked a lot with everyone. When

he lost at cards or something was wrong, he spoke in Polish. I figured he was cussing when he used a language no one else knew.

We had another man who had come from Europe and ended up in the Sixth. His name was Julien Francois. He was a private and very friendly. His tent was near ours and he often sat at the fire writing.

"What are you writing? I asked.

"I make a poem."

"What's it about Julien?"

"It will be about the brave men of the Sixth Wisconsin."

"Were you a poet in France?"

"All Frenchmen are poets, and lovers," he said smiling. He sighed.

"May I read it when it's finished?"

"Of course my young friend. I will be happy to let you read it."

A few weeks later he sat down next to me at the fire. He had a paper in his hands. "Do you still wish to read my poem?"

"Yeah."

He handed it to me.

Chapter 25

Camp Utley, Racine Wisconsin, March 1862

We come from the valleys of the young Badger State,
where the prairies are so grand, so magnificent and great.
We have rallied round the banner of the brave and the free,
around our own starry banner in Dillon's battery.

We have left our homes and the kindred scenes we know well,
while we sniff the pure air of old Lake Michigan.
To perfect ourselves in drill for a time we can be seen,
on our daily rounds of duty in Camp Utley in Racine.

We have got a noble company with officer's true blue,
we will deal out blood and thunder to Jeff Davis and his crew.
We will gather round our banner and stand by it to a man,
when we leave the peaceful shores of old Lake Michigan.

We have banded all together in a just and righteous cause,
and pay homage to the flag they so meanly scorn.
Their forts will be blockaded, their cities we will shell,
we will teach the bloody villains there is a place called hell.

On them we will sight our cannon and try and hold it level,
may God have mercy on them, we will blow them to the

devil.

There is a Price and Ben McCollock we would like to try their metal,
> *and a host of other traitors we have to settle.*

And as we never can expect that the rebel scamps will love us,
> *we would like to see them dangle in the atmosphere above us.*
> *By the prowess of our army and the skill of our profession,*
> *we will rid the land of Dixie of the spirit of secession.*

Let the war cry ring out clearly and the hosts of freedom rally,
> *through the length and the breadth of the Mississippi River valley.*
> *To the friends we leave behind us we will now bid adieu,*
> *we will fight our country's battles with the danger in full view.*

And should it be decreed in the higher courts above,
> *it is a noble boon to die for the country that we love.*
> *Know ye then Wisconsin maidens that to traitors we won't bow,*
> *so gather up your laurels to deck the victor's brow.*

Ere long we shall return and our flag shall be unfurled,
> *the banner of the free and the ages of the world.*
> *Oh we come from the prairies of the young Badger State,*
> *where the girls are so pretty, so amiable and sweet.*

We have rallied round the banner of the brave and the free,
> *around our own starry banner in Dillon's battery.*

I finished reading the poem. Julien looked at me and shrugged.

"Well, Eli, what do you think?"

"It's very good Julien. I think you should show it to Captain Dillon," I said.

"You think?"

"Absolutely."

We passed the poem around the campfire and everyone agreed that it was very good. Julien was happy that we liked it and we talked him into showing it to the Captain.

It soon became a symbol of the men of our battery. To think that it was written by a man who wasn't born in America but came here from France made it all the more special. It showed all of us that our cause was right.

Chapter 26

In February the weather started to warm up a little and the days got a little longer. We still had no idea when we'd be leaving for battle but Captain Dillon and the other officers felt that we needed to do more drills so we'd be ready when it happened.

The gun crews met every day and practiced loading and firing. The livery crews made ready their harnesses and mounts for when they'd hook up the horses and they'd move the cannons. The horsemen exercised the horses and got them ready for a lot of hard work.

Captain Dillon decided that three times a week we would march. The plan was that once we were in the south and moving from town to town, we'd march as we went through the towns on the road. It was thought that it would impress the rebel sympathizers and let them know we were ready and able.

"Eli, you will play a drum cadence to keep the men in step. Foster can you play Yankee Doodle?"

Foster said he knew that one. Preston marched with us carrying his bugle.

There was a large flat field and we cleared the last of the snow off it. Then the officers lined up the men in ranks and Preston, Foster and I were at the head of the ranks. Two or three of the officers were on horseback and when one of them gave the command, I began beating a marching cadence. Every one marched in place. Well they kind of marched in place. There was a lot of laughing and shouting and we stopped and started many times but after a while Captain Dillon gave us the command to march and I began beating a cadence and we stepped off. We actually did fairly well. Of course some of the men had a hard time but most got it.

After we marched across the field Captain Dillon said to turn around and head back and for Foster to play Yankee Doodle. The trip back across the field was better and the fife playing made it all quite festive. We marched back and forth five times and then Captain Dillon decided we were done for the day.

On the way back to our tent I heard some of the men singing Yankee Doodle. I grinned at Foster.

"They like your song," I said.

"I've got to learn some more. That was kind of fun."

The second day of March the officers assembled everyone on the marching field and Captain Dillon was on a horse in front of the group.

"Men, I know everyone is ready to get to the battle and we are ready in every way. I have gotten our orders. We leave Camp Utley on March 15th we will load onto a train and leave for Missouri. We will deploy in St. Louis where we will receive our next orders."

There was a loud cheer. Everyone was sick and tired of marching and practicing. They wanted to shoot the guns at something that might shoot back.

"We have a shipment of uniforms and all of the tents we were missing and in the next week we will have everything we've been waiting for with the exception of all of the big guns we need. I've been promised that we'll have them as soon as we get to St. Louis. It's been a long and cold winter and you've mad a great showing putting up with all the hardships. Now we're off to show the rebels what Wisconsin men are made of."

The men were very excited. The talk around the campfires that night was about the south and putting the fight to the rebels.

I noticed Preston slip off and wondered what was wrong with him. I saw him sitting on the edge of the camp on a log. I walked over by him and sat down.

"What's wrong?"

"We're leaving," he said.

"That's what we've been waiting for."

"I know but I'll be so far from home. How far is it to Missouri?"

"I don't know Preston. It's a long way."

He nodded and I could tell he was homesick.

"You miss your Ma and Pa?"

He nodded.

"We'll be back before you know it. The men say that the south will surrender this spring for sure."

"So we won't be gone that long?"

"I doubt we'll just get settled in and we'll be packing to come back."

He seemed to brighten at that, but little did I know how wrong I was about how long we would be away from Wisconsin.

Chapter 27

I got another letter from Kathy Jane.

My Dearest Eli,

I received your letter and the money. I will put it in a safe place so you can get it when you return. I am so flattered that you thought of me to take care of it for you.

I miss you very much. Every day I pray for you and for your safe return. I think of the walks we took and fishing with you and I hope we can do much more like that when you come home.

We are looking forward to spring here. It's been a long winter. I hope you are well and happy. I think of you all the time.

Miss you,
Kathy Jane

It took nearly all day to load the few guns we had, the horses and everything else that over two hundred men needed for war. It was nearly dark when we finally started south. We'd been issued hardtack and salt pork but the hardtack was so hard we couldn't eat it. Someone got the idea to boil it and that is what we did. When it had been boiled for a while it turned into a big puffball of dough. It wasn't very tasty but at least we could chew it.

We found that we were still missing a lot of equipment when we got to St. Louis. We spent two days there and then moved on to New Madrid. When we got there we found that General Pope had just been victorious and had driven the rebels to Island Number 10. There was a siege in full progress.

We were still only partially equipped so we were held in reserve. It was soon evident that General Pope was so elated over his victory that he cared little for the non-equipped batteries from Wisconsin.

He did find plenty for us to do that didn't involve fighting. Since we had mules and horses he gave us the jobs of moving equipment and when it was impossible for the horses to do the work in marshes and swamps, our men, were put onto long ropes and acted like horses. They were compelled to haul heavy siege guns for miles through the mud, placing them in different points along the riverbank. It didn't take long for the men to become very disappointed with this turn of events.

Eventually we were put in charge of heavy guns that had been placed along the river and were there to prevent re-enforcements or supplies from reaching the besieged rebels on Island Number 10. Our men were involved in several skirmishes and were happy to finally get into the fight.

One day Preston, Foster and I were walking along the riverbank behind the guns just watching what was going on. We came upon an engineering company that was digging entrenchments along the river.

"I'm glad we're musicians," Preston said grinning.

"Remind me not to ever join an engineering company," I said.

Foster stopped and pointed into one of the trenches.

"Look there. There's a black Negro man."

We looked where he was pointing and sure enough.

There was a black Negro man in one of the trenches with two white men and they were all digging. We walked over to watch.

One of the men looked up at us.

"Come to play a tune for us?" he asked smiling.

"Sorry we didn't bring our instruments," I said.

The man noticed we were all looking at the Negro man.

"Never seen a black man before?" he asked.

We all shook our heads no.

"We're from Wisconsin. As far as I know there aren't any Negro men in Wisconsin," Foster said.

The black man looked up and smiled at us.

"My name is Henry Ashby," he said.

"Pleased to meet you Mr. Ashby."

He looked surprised for some reason.

"Did I say something wrong?" I asked.

"In the south, white folks don't call Negro's Mister. They call us boy."

That was surprising. He certainly wasn't a boy, but looked to be around Danny's age, which was around thirty.

"We're boys Sir. That doesn't seem right to call a man a boy."

"How about you call me Henry?"

That seemed fine to us.

We watched them for a while and talked with them. It was getting late in the afternoon so we said goodbye and went back to our camp.

"That was something," Preston said.

"I've seen pictures of black men and women," Foster said, "but he seemed like us cept his skin is black."

"I wonder how he got with that engineering company?" I said.

Meeting the man had been quite an experience. We had no idea we'd ever see him again though.

The rebels finally surrendered from Island Number 10. Captain Dillon didn't wait a minute to call us together and we hurried back to New Madrid and helped ourselves to the guns and all the equipment we were missing that was left behind by the retreating rebels. We were finally fully equipped and ready to do battle wherever we were needed.

Sadly we remained in New Madrid until May 17th.

"Why did we even bother," I asked one evening sitting at the fire with Bruce, Preston, Foster and Danny.

"We'll get in the fight Eli," Bruce said.

"We've been at this for seven months and have barely gotten our guns warm," I said.

"I could be home catching bluegills," Preston said.

"I could go for a few bluegills," Danny said.

"Oh yeah, with some homemade bread and lots of butter."

"And some fresh fried potatoes," Bruce added.

I looked at my ball of dough that I was chewing on.

"Next place we go, we're going to find a place to fish," I said to Preston.

"Do you have any hooks?"

"I bet they have them at the Sutler's tent."

"We'll have to check it out."

The Sutlers were merchants that the government hired to travel with the armies and supply them with their needs. They carried things like socks and gloves and all kinds of things for camp. They also had sweets and tobacco for the men who smoked. Most of the men didn't have much money if they had any at all, so the Sutlers kept a book and charged things to the men. When the men got paid they went and paid their bill and then started over again. Some of the men charged so much, their whole pay was gone and they started out broke every month.

Preston, Foster and I had bought some candy and a few

things like sugar for our oatmeal but we were pretty frugal with our money. I sent some home every month so I'd have something to use when and if I got home.

The next day we loaded everything on transports and proceeded up the Tennessee River to Hamburg Landing. We arrived there on May 23rd. We didn't stay there long and soon we were moved to the main railroad line supplying Corinth. We were put in reserve during the first siege of Corinth. Then we were put under the command of General Pope and participated in the siege for the next several days.

We wanted to get into war. We got our wish. Sadly the siege didn't last very long but we had a taste of battle. On May 26th we moved onto the main rail line going into Cornith and were assigned to General Davis' division. We were with General Pope's forces and when Corinth evacuated, we joined in the pursuit of the rebel retreating forces as far as Boonville. Then we returned to Rienzi where we remained for the rest of the summer.

Chapter 28

Afew days later the three of us were walking to the Sutler's tent to buy some fishing hooks and line. We were talking and not paying too much attention when Foster stopped.

"Look there," he said.

We looked and there was the black man we'd met who was digging trenches. He was wearing a Union uniform and carrying a pail of water toward the officer's tents. We walked over toward him.

"Hello Henry," I called.

He stopped and smiled when he saw us.

"Hello gentlemen. How nice to see you again."

"What are you doing here?" Preston asked.

"Lieutenant Sam Clark asked me to work for him and here I am."

"So you're now part of the Sixth Wisconsin?"

He smiled and nodded.

"I'm adding a little color to a pretty pale unit," he said.

We all laughed.

"So what do you do?"

"I help Lt. Clark with what he needs and when the battles start I'll help supplying the gunners with powder and water and do whatever I can."

Huh.

"Well it's good to see you again. I hope you'll like it here," I said.

"I do already. I've met a lot of very nice friendly people. Wisconsin folks are a lot different than people from the south."

We bid him well and continued to the Sutler's tent.

"I wonder if he knows how to fish?" Preston asked.

Later we had mail call and another letter came from Kathy Jane.

Dear Eli,

Summer is here in full force in Wisconsin. You know how it gets with the warm weather and the big thunderstorms in the evenings. We need some rain Mama says. Our garden is very nice.

How is it there? I bet it's hot there too. Do you have good food? I worry so much every day that you're safe and well. We've heard of some of the men coming down with diseases and of some even dying. I pray every night for you Eli.

I got your last letter and the money you sent. I have it saved in a safe place so you'll have it when you come home. I can hardly wait for that day Eli. I miss you so.

Be safe and be happy.

With great affection,

Kathy Jane

The word was that we'd be near Rienzi for the rest of the summer. Our camp was set up and many of the men set up their tents in little groups and did their own cooking. We were provided salt pork and hardtack and water but not much else. We quickly got tired of salt pork and hardtack.

Preston, Foster, Bruce and I were the three lowest in rank among those in the group we were a part of. We had to be near the officers and they all treated us well. Bruce and Danny had been together from the start so they stayed together after Preston, Foster and I got our own dog tent.

I managed to get an extra tarp and with the supplies I'd brought from Captain Dillon's shop back home, we cut two pieces of tarp to fit on the ends of the dog tent. Then I made buttonholes in the ends of the tent and we sewed buttons on the two flaps so we had a tent that kept us dry and warm.

When we got to a new place, we'd be the ones who set up the tents and made our camp. We made a fire pit and a latrine and then gathered wood to cook over. It was summer now so we weren't worried about cold weather.

When Bruce and Danny saw our new tent they asked us why we wanted to move out of theirs.

"We thought you might be tired of three kids with you," Foster said.

"When we get tired of you, we'll tell you," Bruce said. "Keep your tent up in case we have beans again. Then Preston will have a place to sleep."

The next day we were sitting by the fire warming up in the morning chill.

"We need to go out and forage," Bruce said.

"Forage? What's that mean?"

"It means we go out and find something to eat."

"Where can we find food?"

"We go to the farms and homesteads and take stuff."

"You mean we steal it?"

"The army calls it foraging, but yes, it means we just take what we want."

"What about the people who own it?"

"They're rebels Eli. They don't have any say in it."

That didn't seem right to me but I was pretty darn tired of salt pork and hardtack. So the four of us set out to forage.

We were well behind our lines and there was no fighting so we felt pretty safe. Just in case we kept near the woods and stayed off the main road. We found a farm but it was deserted and there was nothing there.

We saw some smoke coming up through the trees in the woods, and followed it. We found three men sitting by a fire cooking something over the fire. Bruce was carrying his rifle. We snuck close and then stepped out by them. They were pretty scared but we saw they were boys, not much older than me and a little younger than Bruce.

"What are you cooking?" Bruce asked.

The three of them looked at each other and I thought they were going to run away.

"It's a possum."

"Did you shoot it?"

"Ain't got no gun. Chased it down and it played dead and we took a stick and bashed its head in."

I looked at Preston and he made a face.

"You can eat possum?" he asked.

"Heck yeah. Tastes like chicken."

Bruce turned to us. He spoke quietly.

"What do you think?"

"About eating it?"

"About taking it from them."

I looked at Preston and I think he and I both thought it wasn't right to take it away from them. Foster looked really hungry so we figured he was for taking it.

"Maybe we can share it?"

Bruce nodded.

"By rights we can take it from you since you're on the rebel side. But if you'll share it we'll be okay with that," Bruce said.

"Heck yeah, we'll do that."

We sat on the ground by them as the possum finished cooking. It actually smelled pretty good. Of course anything would smell good after what we'd been eating.

"Ya'll are kinda young to be soldiers," one of them said.

"These three are our musicians. He plays the drum and he plays the bugle and that one plays the fife. I'm a Corporal."

"Have you killed anyone?"

"Heck no. We're an artillery battery. We don't shoot regular guns much. We just got into the fight a while ago."

"It's downright decent of ya'll not to take our whole possum."

"We're just looking for something to eat," I said.

"You know where there might be some food?" Preston asked.

"There's some corn down yonder," one said pointing toward the river.

"Go down that road there and there's a house that got burned down by some Yankee soldiers a while back. The people what lived there had a garden but I don't know if they left anything."

That sounded good to us, so Preston and I said we'd go and look and Bruce and Foster stayed to protect our share of the possum.

We found the cornfield. There wasn't much left of it but we managed to find a few ears. I had a cloth bag and we put it in the bag. Then we followed the road and found what was left of the house. The fire had burned the trees around the house and all the grass was dead. It looked pretty bad.

"Don't look like nothing here," Preston said.

"Let's check to be sure."

We found where the garden had been. It was obvious because there wasn't any burnt grass on the ground. We could see where they'd dug the potatoes and other vegetables, and found the bare vines from the tomatoes.

"They took it all," Preston said.

I kicked a lump in the dirt and a potato rolled out. I picked it up.

"We better check closer," I said.

When we left we had seventeen small potatoes, nine carrots and an onion. It wasn't much but Preston said he could make a good stew from it.

"I used to cook with my Ma," he said. "She taught me a lots of stuff."

When we got back the possum was done. The boys split it right down the middle and gave us half.

It smelled really good and our bellies were empty.

"We got some stuff that Preston says he can make stew from," I said.

"If we keep the possum for the stew it will be a lot better," Preston said.

Bruce looked at us and we knew he wanted to take a big chunk of possum and eat it right there.

"Can we have one bite?"

"You're the one in charge," I said.

He shook his head.

"Okay, let's go back. I'm so dang hungry I could eat that whole half a possum."

We said goodbye to the kids and they thanked us again.

When we were halfway back to camp Preston asked Bruce, "Were those guys the enemy?"

"Well technically they're civilians but they're still in the rebel lands. It's kind of hard to think of them as enemies. They were just kids like you guys who were trying to fill their bellies."

"I think sharing with them was good," I said.

"Just don't tell the others. They'll think we're soft."

We promised to keep the secret.

Chapter 29

W hen we got back Bruce went to the cook tent and borrowed a big kettle with a handle on it and a steel tripod that we could put over our fire. I helped Preston clean the corn up and take it off the cobs. It was hard and didn't look very tasty.

"We need something to crush it up and then we'll boil it for a while to soften it up," he said.

Bruce found a big flat stone and we got a hammer and smashed up the corn. We put it in the pot and filled it about half way up with water. Preston said we needed some salt and pepper so Bruce went looking. He came back a while later with a little bag of each.

Meanwhile Preston and I cleaned the potatoes, carrots and onion. We cut the potatoes and carrots in small pieces and sliced the onion very thin into ribbons. Preston picked every scrap of meat off the possum carcass and put the bones in the stew pot.

We let it cook for twenty minutes and then he fished the bones out. We put in the potatoes and carrots and onion and soon it was bubbling and it smelled really good.

"Can you take some hardtack and break it up with the hammer?" he asked.

"I surely can do that," I said.

I smashed up several pieces of hardtack. Preston tasted the stew and added salt and pepper and nodded.

"Not bad," he said.

He got a spoonful and I tasted it.

"Holy cats, that's good!"

He let Bruce taste it and he was smiling from ear to ear.

"How soon can we eat it?"

"I'm going to put the pieces of hardtack in and let them soften up and make it thicker. Tell the others to bring their plates."

A few minutes later the officers gathered around and Preston dished each of them a plate of stew. Captain Dillon waited until last and when he got this food he smiled at us.

"You've been busy," he said.

"We don't have much to do except blow a few calls and drum now and then. We might as well be useful," I said.

Well to say the stew went over well was an understatement. The men all raved at how good it was. They ate every drop of it.

"What was that meat?" Danny asked.

Bruce looked at Preston and me and winked.

"Chicken," he said.

"Boy that was tasty. I think we should make you three permanent cooks for our group."

They all thought that was a good idea.

Captain Dillon nodded and smiled. I think he was pretty proud of us.

That night in the tent everyone was in good spirits. Danny read to us from the Bible, and told us the story of Daniel in the lion's den.

"The other officers were talking about putting some money together so we could get what you need to cook more meals like that," Bruce said. "We thought you could go to the Sutler's tent and buy spices and things and we'd have better chow."

We thought that was a good idea and it gave Preston, Foster and me a chance to be of use.

"I won't be able to go with you all the time, but you three are pretty clever. I don't think you'll get in any trouble as long as you stay behind our lines."

"We'll be careful," I said.

The next morning my pals and I went and bought sugar and cinnamon and several pots and a flat steel griddle. We bought a couple of cooking spoons and a spatula and Preston was pretty sure he could make us some good meals. We also bought a bag of rolled oats that he wanted to make for our breakfast the next day.

"Hardtack and side pork aren't breakfast," he said.

"Hardtack and side pork aren't much for any meal except to fill an empty belly. Should we go looking now?"

He nodded.

"Let's get some fishing hooks and some line and go down by the river. Maybe we can catch some fish for supper."

Boy, that sounded like a good idea and a lot of fun.

An hour later we'd each cut a long willow for a pole and had tied a piece of string on it. We turned over some logs and found some worms. We each cut a little dry stick for a float and bent a little piece of wire around our line above our hook for a sinker. We were in a river slough where there were lilies and reeds and it looked like a place to catch bluegills.

We took off our shoes and socks and sat in the sun. In the distance we could hear the guns and cannons firing.

"It's hard to believe that there's a war going on," I said.

"Yeah it is. We really haven't been in much of a fight yet. Do you think we'll just be in reserve for the whole rest of the war?"

"I know Captain Dillon is itching to get to the fight but I don't know. He has to take orders from the General."

"Well at least we don't have to worry about getting shot."

The sun got hot and we took off our coats. Our uniforms were made of wool and they were very hot in the mid-day sun.

I took off my shirt.

"Let's take a swim," Preston suggested.

"We'll scare the fish."

"Have you caught a fish?"

"Well no."

"We can move over there," he said pointing to a higher bank with a big tree on it.

We got up and walked over and took off our pants and stood there in our underwear. He looked at me and grinned and then he took off his underwear and jumped off the bank into the water. He came up laughing and splashing me.

"Come in it's great."

I pulled off my underwear and jumped in too. Foster was right behind me. The water was cool and it felt great. It had been a while since we'd had a bath and we needed it. We swam and laughed and after a while we got our uniforms and washed them out in the water. We hung them on branches to dry.

"Now what?"

"Well let's see if the fish are biting. Maybe we woke them up when we were swimming," I said.

We walked over and baited up and threw out. I looked at Preston and Foster and we grinned.

"I hope none of our men come down here and see us naked," he said.

"I hope no rebels sneak up on us and take us prisoner," Foster added.

Chapter 30

Our clothes were dry so we dressed and headed back to camp. We didn't catch any fish but we planned on looking for a better spot the next day. That night we had hardtack and salt pork.

"We gotta find something tomorrow," Preston said. "We'll be fired as cooks if we feed them hardtack again."

There were a lot of the men who were sick. Danny said it was from drinking bad water. They'd eat something and it would go right through them. I mean right through. Some got so sick they had to be taken to the hospital.

Some of the others had something Danny called sypha-something. I asked him what it was and he said it was from being too friendly with loose women. Preston, Foster and I didn't know what that meant. We asked Bruce and he said he'd tell us when we were older.

"Oh come on," Preston said.

"We're not little babies. We're soldiers," I said.

Bruce grinned.

"Do you guys know about babies?"

"Babies? What's babies got to do with anything?"

"Do you know how babies are made?"

I looked at Preston. I wasn't too sure, but I didn't want him to know that. Foster grinned. He knew.

"You know don't you?" I asked.

He nodded but he looked at Bruce to tell us.

"Well, you know how boys and girls are different?" Bruce

asked.

"You mean like boys wear pants and girls wear dresses?"

"Well no, not that. You know how they look down there," he said pointing down.

We looked down at his feet.

"We wear work shoes and they wear girl shoes," Preston said.

Bruce shook his head.

"I mean here."

He pointed where his pants met his shirt.

"Oh!"

"You know the difference."

We both nodded. We'd been told about it but didn't have first hand experience. Foster was having a hard time not to laugh.

"Well the man and the woman get together."

Preston and I chewed on that for a bit. Then he nodded like he understood. He made a circle with his thumb and finger and put his other finger in the circle.

"Ah," I said. Now I got it.

"Well some of these ladies in the towns where we go near, have a sickness in that area. And if the men get with them, you know, they catch the sickness."

"You mean they get it on their... down there?"

He nodded.

"Is it bad?"

"It can kill you."

I looked at Preston. That didn't sound very good.

"We'll stay clear of those women," Preston said.

Bruce laughed.

"That's a good idea. So are you guys going to catch some fish tomorrow?"

"Dang, I hope so."

It was still really nice. It was late September and the air was still warm but not so hot like it had been. There was fighting every day and our men fired some volleys but a big battle hadn't happened for a while. It was like they were just keeping the inside of the gun barrels from getting full of cobwebs. We were expecting a big battle and a siege in a few weeks.

As we walked through the camp we heard many of the little groups of men complaining about doing nothing but drill and clean the guns.

"We might as well stayed in Wisconsin," one said as we walked past.

"Least we'd have something to do worthwhile," another said.

While it was exciting to think of being in battle with all the noise and shooting, it was a little scary too. So far we'd had a few of our men injured but no one had been killed. A couple had died of sickness, so we hoped that our good luck would last.

"What do you think?" Preston asked me.

"About getting into the fight?"

He nodded.

"I guess we came all this way and did all this practicing, it would seem that we'd have a better use than just sitting around."

"But leastwise we're not getting shot," Foster said.

"True, but it seems like that General doesn't much think we're worth much," I said.

"I heard Captain Dillon talking to the officers and they think we'll be in the battle soon."

I wasn't sure if that was a good thing or not.

Preston made oatmeal with a little cinnamon and sugar in it for breakfast. He was the most popular guy in the camp.

Chapter 31

Preston, Foster and I took our fishing gear and headed toward the river. We figured we'd find a spot and maybe we'd catch some fish. It was pretty safe because we were on the backside of our lines. We had to watch though because sometimes Rebels snuck through. We didn't want to run into any of them.

We found a nice spot by a big tree that had fallen into the river. We sat on the bank by it and put our hooks in the water. We hadn't been at it very long and Preston caught a catfish. Then I caught a bluegill. Foster caught a bluegill too. Then we started catching fish one after another.

We had a piece of twine along and strung it through the fish's gill and put them in the water to keep them fresh. We'd brought some worms with us but we ran out pretty fast.

"We got to go find worms," I said.

We put our poles down and went into the woods. We looked for logs and limbs lying on the ground and rolled them over. We'd find worms under most of them and grab them and then put them into the can.

We had just rolled a log over and we heard a voice.

"Come on, we have to do it. Daddy said not to come back with him."

Then we heard another younger voice crying.

"Why can't he stay?"

"We can't barely feed us. There's nothing for him to eat."

We looked through the brush and saw two black boys.

They both were wearing bib overalls and were barefoot. One had on a white shirt and the other a light blue shirt. The older one was wearing a straw hat. They were walking along and the little one was pulling on a rope. The older one looked about our age.

"What are they pulling?" Preston whispered.

"I don't know. Should we let them see us?"

"I don't think they'd hurt us. We're big as that one and bigger than the other."

We gathered up our can and stood up. They were a little nearer the river so we followed behind them. We were twenty feet back when the little guy heard us and turned.

He started screaming and running through the woods.

"Wait, we won't hurt you," I shouted.

The older one looked really scared. We were wearing our uniforms. They thought we were soldiers.

"We're not going to hurt you," Preston said.

"Jimmy, it's okay," the older one said. The little kid looked from behind a tree.

We walked up to them.

"Ya'll ain't soldiers are ya'll?"

"We're musicians. I play the drum and Preston plays the bugle, and Foster plays the fife," I said.

"Are ya'll foraging?"

"We're fishing," I said.

The little guy came up by us. He was pulling a puppy along through the brush.

"They just like us... kids," the older one said.

"Ya'll got anything to eat?"

I felt in my pocket and had a couple of pieces of penny candy that I'd planned on sucking on later. I handed him one and offered the other to the big boy.

"What's your name?" I asked.

"I'm Ben and that little guy is Jimmy. How bout ya'll?"

DRUMMER

"I'm Eli and this is Preston and that guy is Foster."

"Ya'll catchin' any fish?"

"Yeah, they're biting good. We ran out of worms."

"Huh. We fished some. Lost all our hooks. Got no money go buy more."

I looked at Preston. He grinned.

"We got some extras. Come on we'll rig you up and we can all fish."

The two of them looked kind of surprised but followed along with us.

We walked to the riverbank. Jimmy was still very sad acting.

"Don't you want to fish?"

He looked at the little dog and shook his head. '

"My Daddy said I have to take Crumb down to the river and tie a rock on his rope and drown him."

"What? Why?"

"We ain't got no food what to feed him."

I looked at the pup. He was small and had big floppy ears. His little tail wagged and he licked my hand.

"What if you brought some fish home? Would they let you keep him then?"

"He said don't come back with no dog."

I looked at Preston and Foster and they knew what I was thinking.

"We'll get in trouble," Foster said.

"Oh come on. We need a good guard dog in camp."

He grinned.

"What's he gonna guard against, mosquitoes?"

"We can't let him get drowned."

"Oh boy."

Chapter 32

"Jimmy, what if I take him back with me? I'll promise to take good care of him and he'll have a good home."

"Then I wouldn't have to drown him?"

"No, I know you'll still miss him but at least he'll have a life."

He smiled. His face lit up and he nodded yes.

"I'd like that. I'd really like that," he said.

"What did you say his name was?"

"His name be Crumb."

"Crumb, like from toast?"

He nodded.

"He was the runt of the litter and not much bigger than a crumb, so that's what we called him. But times is hard. Our master and his family are gone and left us to take care of the place but they didn't leave us any food. What little we had got took by some other soldiers a week or so back. We got no food for us so Daddy said he had to go."

"Well we'll be good to him and see to it he's got a good place to sleep and food," Preston said.

"He'll be a Yankee though," Foster added grinning.

"Heck I don't care what he's a Yankee or not I just don't want him to be dead."

We rigged up two more poles and sat side-by-side with Ben and Jimmy. We caught fish all afternoon and then we took a swim. Crumb came in the water with us and we had a fine time.

It was getting late in the afternoon so we divided up the fish.

"Ya'll are gonna let us have these?"

"Sure you caught that many."

"Ya'll know, we're rebels. We're the enemy."

I looked at Preston and Foster and we grinned. They didn't seem like an enemy to us. They were just a couple of kids.

"Then we just won't tell anyone."

Jimmy hugged Crumb and he cried some more. I promised him he could visit any time.

We let them keep the fishing poles and gave them a couple extra hooks and said goodbye. When we were nearly back at camp Preston stopped.

"It's kind of hard to figure out this rebel and union thing. Those guys were just kids like us but if they got in the wrong place they'd probably get shot. And if you and I walked in the wrong place we'd probably get shot too."

"Crazy isn't it?"

When we got to camp there was a lot of commotion. There had been quite a lot of shelling during the day and everyone was pretty excited. Then they saw our stringer of fish and they knew they'd have something besides hardtack and side pork for dinner.

"And what it that?" Bruce asked.

"That's our new guard dog."

"Guard dog. What's it guard against, mice?"

"He'll grow. He's just a pup."

Bruce squatted down by the little guy and he licked his hand. He grinned at him and I knew we had Bruce on our side.

"What about Captain Dillon?" he asked.

"I thought you'd maybe convince him that a dog would be good for guard duty and stuff."

"And stuff."

I nodded.

Bruce shook his head.

"Keep him out of sight until after he has a fish dinner. Then he'll be easier to talk to."

Crumb was ready for a nap anyway, so we put him in the tent. He nosed his way into a pile of blankets and in no time he was snoring. We had plenty of help cleaning fish. Some of the men had found a potato patch and had enough of them that we could slice them up and fry them to go with the fish. Nobody would get a lot of them but a taste was better than nothing. When the potatoes were nearly done Preston got a couple of big frying pans and began frying fish. We were pretty popular.

Danny came back from the guns and crawled into the tent. Suddenly we heard him shouting and he came crawling out backwards.

"There's a critter in there," he said. "I didn't see what it was but I think it was some kind of rat."

Bruce and the three of us began laughing.

"It's a dog. It's only a puppy," I said as I crawled in and got Crumb.

"What the heck is a dog doing in there?"

"He's the new guard dog."

"Oh?"

I turned and Captain Dillon was standing nearby.

"We were just going to talk to you about this weren't we Preston?"

Preston gave me the evil eye.

"I'm listening."

We told him the story. He took Crumb from my arms. He held him up and looked at him. Crumb's tongue came out and got him right on the lips.

"If he barks and wakes me up."

"He won't."

He handed him back to me. I grinned at Preston, Foster and Bruce. Danny just shook his head.

136

Chapter 33

Many of the men were restless and wanted to move somewhere where there was some fighting going on but my two best buddies and I were having a good time. We'd go fishing almost every day and most days we came back to camp with plenty of fish. Some of the men chipped in a little money for us to buy extras for cooking and Preston was very good at making new things with very little ingredients. He did most of the cooking and Foster and I were the helpers.

We'd make a dinner of whatever we'd caught or someone had foraged and then everyone in our part of the camp would get a share and we'd all sit and eat.

One evening Foster got his fife and began playing some songs on it. The men were very appreciative. Then someone asked if he'd play *Yankee Doodle* and he said yes. He told me to get my drum and I played along with him while he played the song. Soon many of the men were singing with us.

I noticed Captain Dillon sitting on a campstool near his tent with a smile on his face. His hand was tapping on his knee to the song.

Foster knew a lot of songs. I didn't know he was as good as he turned out to be. He played *Old Folks At Home* and many sang along. Some of the men had tears in their eyes as they sang. To liven things up Foster played *Camptown Races*. That got everyone singing and a few of the men got up and danced.

When we finished we were walking to our tent and Captain Dillon stopped me.

"Thank you and Foster for that," he said.

"It was fun huh?"

"Moral is very important in the military. We've been sitting on our hands for a quite a while and the men are restless. That little show you guys put on made them forget about the monotony of war and the waiting for a while."

"We'll have to do it more from now on," I said.

He ruffled my hair and turned into his tent. I stood there for a minute. Captain Dillon was a very special man. When I had nothing and no one he took me in and made me feel needed and wanted. He was like a second father to me. I felt pretty good as I snuggled down in my blankets in our tent. Crumb crawled in with me and sighed.

The next day we got mail again. I got another letter from Kathy Jane.

Dear Eli,

I hope you are well and happy. We had a nice 4th of July celebration but it would have been much happier if our men were here. It was mostly women, children and old men. Tom asked if I'd heard from you and I told him you weren't much of a letter writer but that you had written and were sending money back. He said that was a good thing and to tell you, Preston and Foster hello.

I've been going over and riding Franklin nearly every day. He's a very gentle horse and I thought if I kept him used to being ridden he's stay that way.

Otherwise I help Mama at the store and sit and think of you Eli. I miss you so much. I know that you're being careful but please be extra careful. I don't know what I'd do if something happened to you.

With love,
Kathy Jane.

"You seem to get a letter from that girl pretty regularly," Bruce said as I sat and read my mail.

I folded it up quickly and knew my face turned red.

"She's just a friend," I said.

"She's a girl. She's a friend. So that means she's a girlfriend."

"She's not my girlfriend Bruce."

"Have you kissed her?"

My face got really hot. Bruce broke out in a wide grin.

"You have! Eli, you dog!"

I got up and went in the tent. Jeez.

I thought about Kathy Jane. I'd known her for a long time and for most of that time I just thought of her as a pest with pigtails. But here lately before we left for the war, she quit having pigtails and her hair looked pretty nice. She wasn't so skinny anymore either and had curves in places she hadn't had them before. She wasn't such a pest either.

"I really should send her a letter other than with some money and hello," I thought.

I thought about her and I walking barefoot in the wet sand at the river. I remembered how she held my hand. Dang.

Dear Kathy Jane,

Thanks for your letters. I'm not much of a letter writer as you know. But I do like hearing about home.

Of course for me there isn't very much at home any more since my family is gone. But there is Tom and the Dillon family that mean a lot and you too of course. I actually had fun taking you fishing and stuff. I hope we can do that some more when I get home.

Oh we have a dog. His name is Crumb. We got him from some black kids what had to drown him because their daddy said they couldn't afford to feed him. He was just a little booger but he's growing pretty fast. We had to talk Captain

Dillon into letting us keep him but now he's the camp mascot. I'll bring him home when I come home. You'll like him.

Please say hi to Tom from all three of us. He'd be proud of us, and how well his music lessons helped us and now we even play evenings around the campfires to keep up the moral of the men.

Well I have to get to work here. We have lots to do every day and the word is that we'll soon be in battle again. I hope to see you soon. Thanks for taking care of my money.

Your really good friend,
Eli

Chapter 34

The next morning there was a lot of activity around Captain Dillon's headquarters. All of the officers were there and it seemed that something important was going to happen. I saw Bruce there standing in the back taking it all in and watched until he glanced my way. I shrugged my shoulders like I was asking what was happening. He nodded and let me know he'd tell me later.

When the meeting broke up Bruce came over by the guys and me. He picked up Crumb and ruffled him.

"He's growing," he said.

"He gets a lot of food being the only dog in camp," I said. "A lot of the men have dogs at home that they miss, so they feed him all the time. He'll be a big boy soon. So what's going on?"

"We're moving back to Corinth. The rebels have established a garrison there and we have to go back and route them out again."

"So will we get to fight this time?" Preston asked.

"We're under General Hamilton and it looks like we'll be on a ridge over the town to fire on the rebels and hold the ridge."

The three of us looked at one another and I could tell everyone was excited. We experienced little combat and were tired of just sitting around and waiting for something to happen. We knew the men were itching to get into a fight too.

The camp was full of activity as tents came down and guns were prepared for the move. The gunnery crews made the guns ready with a thing called a Limber Pole. It was attached to the gun and then it was hooked to six horses that would pull the thing. Two soldiers rode the front two horses on the right side. There was a Limber Box on the rig and it held fuse and things needed for shooting the gun. Some of the soldiers rode on the box too.

By mid-afternoon the unit was ready to begin the move. Captain Dillon had Preston blow the bugle call for marching out and when we got going, Foster and I played *Yankee Doodle* as we started down the road. Everyone was very excited and happy to finally be doing something besides drill and wait.

We arrived outside Corinth just at dusk. Some officers from General Hamilton's camp met us and showed us where to put our camp and where to mount our guns for the siege.

The guns were just left on the Limber poles for the night and the horses unhooked and taken care of, while the rest of the unit set up tents and made the camp ready. It was late by the time we had the tents up. We built campfires and heated up some salt pork and hardtack as it was about all we had time to fix for supper.

Preston, Foster and I were already looking for places to fish and maybe for a place to hunt for some squirrels. Now that we'd had some better food, we were not too fond of hardtack any more.

Preston blew reveille at dawn and the camp slowly came to life. Fires were stoked for morning coffee and the gun crews got their guns ready for the assault that was to happen the next morning.

"According to this map there's a small river to the north," Bruce said to us. "Captain Dillon thought you guys might try for some fish."

"Is it safe?"

"It should be. All the rebels are south of us. I'll let you take a Sharps carbine with you just in case."

"Really? We can take a gun?"

"It's just in case. You guys know how to shoot don't you?"

We all nodded yes.

"I've shot squirrels and rabbits for a long time," Preston said.

Foster and I said we'd hunted too.

"Well if you happen to run past a squirrel or rabbit, bring it home too," Bruce said.

"Or a possum," Foster said.

We got our fishing lines and hooks and Bruce gave us a rifle and some cartridges. We felt pretty important as we headed out looking for the river.

It took a while to get to the river but we found it with no trouble. We'd brought Crumb with us and he got all excited when we rolled over logs in the woods. He'd dig in the damp earth with his paws trying to help us. We found some worms and then we cut three willow branches for poles. We rigged up and sat on a bank with a nice grassy spot and began fishing.

"Do you think we'll get some action tomorrow?" Foster asked.

"We're not in reserve this time. General Pope didn't seem to hold much stock in us northern boys," I said.

"Are you scared?" Preston asked.

"Not really. We've not been in any big battles but we've done some shooting. We've had a few men wounded so it's not like we've been doing nothing."

"We've lost more men to sickness than anything," Foster said.

Just then Preston got a bite and caught a bass. That was pretty exciting. We put it on a string and hung it in the water and in no time we began catching more bass, bluegills and a few perch. We were having great fun fishing, when Foster stopped and listened intently

"What?"

"Did you hear that?"

"What?"

"I heard a horse."

We looked around. There was a knoll a little way off and we snuck over that way and peeked up over the top. There were two young men leading a horse along the riverbank. They weren't wearing uniforms but were just wearing regular clothes.

"Suppose they're rebels?" Preston whispered.

"Don't know."

"We should lay low."

We all nodded. We lay in the tall grass and watched. They walked along watching the trees.

"They're hunting," Preston whispered.

They looked like they were just a little older than us. One of them had a rifle. The other was just along with him.

"Ya'll think we're getting too far from camp?"

"Don't know. We've walked a bit. Don't want to get too close to the Union boys."

"We better start heading south. We got to be far enough from their camp."

"Look!"

They were looking up in a tree near us. There was a red squirrel running across a branch. The guy with the rifle pulled up and aimed for a long time and then he shot. The squirrel dropped just ten feet from us.

They came hurrying over to pick up their squirrel.

"Dang, they're gonna see us," Preston said urgently.

"Stay still!"

The two picked up the squirrel and looked pretty happy.

"We should skin it and eat it right here," one said.

"Cant' build no fire. The boys in blue will see it."

"True."

Crumb had been watching everything and he couldn't stand it any longer. He ran out toward the two guys wagging his tail.

"Look at that!"

"Wonder where that little guy came from?" one of them said.

Just then their horse smelled us or noticed us. It bolted and the guy holding the rope around its neck held onto it but noticed Foster lying in the grass.

"Somebody's there!"

The other one pulled up the rifle and pointed it at us.

"Ya'll better show yerself."

Preston had the rifle. He gripped it and stood up holding it right toward the two guys.

"We don't mean you no harm," he said.

Foster and I stood up too.

"Dang how many are there of ya'll?"

"Just us."

"What are ya'll doin' here?"

"We're fishing."

"Ya'll are Union soldiers."

"We're musicians," I said. "We play the drums and stuff."

The two of them looked at each other.

"Why ya'll got a gun?"

"We hoped to get a squirrel or rabbit. But you got it first," Preston said.

The two of them grinned. We could see now that they weren't much older than we were.

"So what now?" one asked.

The three of us looked at each other.

"Don't rightly know. We'll go back to fishing and you go where you were going."

They looked at each other and that seemed to please them. The one with the gun lowered it and Preston lowered our gun.

"Are you rebels?" Foster asked.

"Heck yeah."

"Why don't you have uniforms?"

"Lots of us don't have none. Some don't even have any shoes."

"Times are tough," I said.

"Heck yeah. Well we'll be headin' back now."

"I'd go a little farther east," I said. "The way you're heading you might get a little close to our unit."

"Much obliged."

They started off to the east.

"Are you going to Corinth?" I asked.

"Yep."

"Not a good idea," I said to Foster and Preston.

We had a lot of fish but no squirrels or rabbits. Several men helped clean the fish and Preston began frying them. I took the rifle to Bruce.

"We ran into a couple of rebels," I said.

"Did they see you?"

I nodded.

"They were hunting squirrels."

"You didn't shoot them?"

I grinned

"They were about the same age as us. Didn't see no reason to shoot them for just hunting squirrels," I said.

"What happens if tomorrow you're on the ridge with your drum and one of them sees you and puts a bullet through your head?"

"Then I guess I'll wish I'd have shot them. But, I don't think that's going to happen."

"No one thinks they're going to die tomorrow. We've been

lucky. We've had some of the unit die from diseases but no one's been killed. The odds are that one of these days, we'll have casualties."

That was kind of sobering. I looked around the camp and wondered if anyone I was looking at might be the one. I had no idea what the next day was going to bring.

Chapter 35

On the morning of October 3, 1862, Preston didn't play reveille. The night before, word was passed through the camp that everyone would be woken up when the officers passed word that it was time to get ready for the assault. Everyone was up and had a quick breakfast and then everyone moved to his place along the firing line. We were on the end of a sloping ridge above the town of Corinth. It wasn't much of a town being only about two thousand people. We'd been here earlier in the war but that time we were in reserve and hadn't seen much action. Now under General Hamilton, we had a line of artillery trained on the rebel encampment in and around the town.

It was clear and cool on top of the ridge. Below in the valley the fog still hung over the town and the rebels. Captain Dillon was on the upper part of the ridge with several of the other officers and Captain Hood was on the lower end with the rest. In between the guns were ready and the men was excited about getting into some real fighting.

We'd taken our positions on the ridge quietly so as not to warn the rebels. Our men were ready. Captain Dillon looked down the ridge and nodded to me. I began playing a drum roll. I started softly and made the sound louder and louder. Then Captain Dillon nodded to Preston and he blew the bugle call to fire.

The morning stillness was shattered when the guns began going off. One after another they fired at the valley and the rebels. Below us in the town the shells landed and exploded. I saw houses get hit and begin burning. I saw men running. Our crews fired and once they fired, the crews reloaded and fired again.

The officers watched the shells strike and called out to gun crews to change their elevation or to aim more to the left or right. Those who usually took care of the horses or had other jobs carried rifles and filled in between gunnery crews firing down the hill toward the enemy, now scurrying around, trying to get organized so they could fight back.

Bruce was with us near Captain Dillon. He was very excited and yelled encouragement.

"They'll send their infantry soon," he said to me. "Then we'll have to drive them back."

I saw Henry Ashby carrying powder up the hill. Then he ran back down and carried up more powder and soon he was carrying water for the crews. He ran back and forth many times and didn't seem to be worried about getting hit. Later I saw him carrying a rifle and firing down the hill. He was really a part of it.

Soon the guns from the town began firing up at us. Some hit short but after a few of those short shots they got their aim zeroed in and shells began landing closer to us. One of our guns was hit and disabled and two of the gunners were injured but not bad enough to be fatal.

Some of the men carrying rifles carried the injured men down the backside of the hill to the doctors to work on. Rifle shots soon began ringing out from below. I saw a man I knew named Gilbert Thomas who was only nineteen years old, get hit with a bullet and drop. He didn't move and I was pretty sure he was dead. A bit later George Brown, who was age twenty also got shot, and when he fell he looked like he wasn't getting up again either. Things were getting pretty scary now. A few of our men got hit and were only wounded and were taken to the field hospital. Henry Ashby always seemed to be right there to help carry the wounded too. He was everywhere at once it seemed. The sound of bullets zipping through the air made us keep our heads down, and while it was very exciting to be in battle, it also was dangerous.

"We're in it now," Foster said.

"We got our wish."

We fired at the town and the rebels fired back all morning. We could hear other units to the east and west of us doing the same. The plan was to push the rebels south and out of the area and then run them down and finish them off. It was important for us to keep our line and not let them break through.

Lieutenant Danny came low walking over by us.

"Captain Dillon asked me to see if you guys can round up something for the men to eat."

"Everybody?"

"Well, he thought maybe some oatmeal or something that we've got a lot of. You're pretty good at making it taste pretty good. Maybe you could go and help the cooks fix it up so it tastes a little better."

"Don't he need us to signal?"

"We're just going to keep shooting all day unless the rebels wave a white flag and we don't think that's going to happen."

"So you want us to be cooks?" Preston asked.

Danny grinned.

"Hey, I'd do it but nobody would eat my cooking. Don't tell the other cooks I said this but you guys are way better cooks than they are."

"I don't guess we got much else to do," I said.

"Thanks boys. Where's Crumb?"

"We left him by our tent with a bowl of water. We thought

he might get shot if we brought him up here."

"Good idea. He'll be happy to see you guys while you cook."

We were a little disappointed but we really weren't of much use crouching below the crest of the hill. I was getting a little tired of the dang cannons going off anyway.

We went down to the camp and got a bunch of big pots from the cook tent and built a fire in the fire pit. There was an iron grate on top of it and we measured out oatmeal and water and began boiling it. The regular cooks worked with us, and when the oatmeal was almost ready Preston dug into his box of stuff and came out with brown sugar, cinnamon and some molasses and added a bit to each pot. After it had cooked for a while we tasted it and it was pretty darn good. A couple of the horse handlers rigged up a wagon and a couple of horses and we took it up behind the hilltop and the men brought their tin plates down and we filled each of them with the oatmeal. They were all real happy with it and we got a lot of thanks.

When we got to where the officers were, Preston went up and collected their plates and we filled them and then the three of us carried them up.

Captain Dillon smiled widely when he saw us.

"What would we do without you boys?" he asked.

"We're happy to do what we can," Foster said.

We fed all of the men and there was a bit left for us and Crumb got a nice dish full too. We helped clean up the pots and walked back up. The firing went on all day long and when it got dark both sides stopped.

Sentries were posted and the bulk of the men came down off the hill to rest and cook their hardtack and salt pork.

"Too bad we didn't have a bunch of fish or squirrels," I said.

"That would be a heck of a bunch of fish to feed this whole

dang bunch," Preston said.

Campfires sprang up around the camp and the men gathered in little groups, talking about the day and tomorrow. We got our instruments and played for a while but everyone was pretty tired so we crawled into our tent.

"Poor George and Gilbert got killed," I said.

"There was lots of bullets flying," Preston said.

"I wonder if we got any rebels?" Foster asked.

"Most likely. We caught them sleeping."

"They won't be sleeping tomorrow," I said.

"They'll be waiting for us, for sure."

Chapter 36

That night Bruce sat down by us and said that Captain Dillon had asked if we'd get up early and make oatmeal for the men so they could eat before they went up on the ridge. Bruce said he'd wake us and help get the food ready so we said we'd be happy to do whatever helped.

"It was exciting today huh?" he asked.

"It was better than drilling and cleaning guns all day," Foster said.

"Tomorrow we'll finish them off. They can't take another day of shelling."

"So tomorrow it will be over?" I asked.

Bruce nodded.

It was still very dark when Bruce woke us. I heard my name and opened my eyes.

"Get up, time to make oatmeal."

I yawned and stretched. Someone farted. The three of us started giggling.

"What a pig!" Preston said.

"It wasn't me, it came from your side of the tent," Foster said.

"Crumb, bad dog!" Preston said.

We laughed and laughed as we dressed. We crawled out into the damp night air. Crumb ran over to a tree and peed.

"I got to do that too," I said.

We went down by the big fire pit and Bruce was there, building a cooking fire. The regular cooks were measuring out water and oatmeal. The three of us helped get the oatmeal ready and put the pots on the fire to cook. Bruce went to the officer's tents and told them breakfast would be ready in a few minutes and then he began waking soldiers up. Everyone was told to be quiet and not make a lot of noise to wake the rebels on the other side of the hill.

Everyone came by for a plate of oatmeal. We'd made coffee too and they were glad for that. When everyone was filled up we ate and fed Crumb. We cleaned up the pots and tied Crumb to a tree by the tent with a pan of water. Most of the unit was already up on the hill getting their guns loaded and everything ready.

The excitement was so thick you could feel it. In the east, the sky began to turn orange. Captain Dillon told me to do a drum roll and I started beating it out on my drum. Then he signaled to Preston to play the fire at will bugle call. Preston blew the call and the guns began firing. The still morning turned into a deafening roar and the sweet night air was filled with gunpowder.

It was October 4, 1862, and we felt like we were invincible. We'd been in the army for over a year and had lost a few men to illness and had only two had been killed in the fighting. We had the rebels right where we wanted them and there was little doubt we'd mop them up in no time.

When the sun came up enough to let us see down into the valley we were surprised. The handful of guns and soldiers had multiplied during the night. There were many more guns, thousands more soldiers and hundreds of horses.

I walked over by Bruce who was crouching next to a gun.

"There's a lot more of them today," I said.

"No matter. We'll take them. It'll just take longer."

The fighting raged on all morning. It was much fiercer than the day before and there were a lot more rebel soldiers shooting at us. There was a huge battle farther up the hill to the left. It sounded like a large number of rebels had broken through the lines next to us and suddenly we looked and all we could see was Confederate soldiers coming down the ridge toward us. We looked to the right and another group of rebels was flanking us on that side too.

Captain Dillon and the other officers ordered our riflemen to defend the position and several of our gunners turned their guns toward the rebels and began fighting. Bruce was running back and forth shooting and shouting at the men where to shoot.

Suddenly a Confederate officer appeared on the hill above us. He had a single star on his cap and he ran forward holding a Confederate flag over one of our guns.

"This battery is mine!" he shouted.

The scene seemed to slow down in my mind. I saw Bruce look at the man holding the flag and he shook his head back and forth.

"Oh no it is not!" he yelled.

Then he ran up to the officer and shot him dead. There were dozens of rebels surrounding Bruce.

"Bruce! Get out of there!" I screamed.

The rebels fired and Bruce was cut down in a hail of bullets. I watched as he fell, lifeless to the ground. Preston grabbed me and pulled me back down over the crest of the hill. I didn't realize that I was still screaming until we fell and rolled down the hill.

"We've got to go back and help Bruce!" I yelled.

"We can't help Bruce, he's dead."

I looked at Preston and Foster and they were both crying. I knew our friend was gone.

Bullets began whistling past us. We ran behind some

trees and I saw one of our boys from Lone Rock, George Barney fall.

Our boys fought bravely and gained ground on the rebels. I saw many of the men get hit. Some fell and others fought on. The battle raged for hours and for a while I thought we were going to be overrun.

Captain Dillon rallied the men and soon there was fierce fighting. Then I saw Lieutenant Danny Noyes, our great friend get hit in the leg. Danny fell and tried to crawl to safety and a Confederate officer ran up to him and bayoneted him while he lay there on the ground. The officer stabbed him over and over.

When our men saw Danny die, a great roar went up and they began to fight like madmen. They recaptured the lost ground and drove the rebels off the hill. They returned to their guns and fired relentlessly into the valley. Several hours later the rebels surrendered.

Other units on either side of us rallied to us and rounded up the rebels and took control of their guns.

When the bullets stopped flying, we walked up onto the hill. The three of us walked slowly to where Bruce lay. He was lying on his back, his blue eyes staring up at the sky. Those blue eyes that sparkled with mischief so many times... now were lifeless.

Tears ran down my face. Bruce had been there for me when my family died and if it hadn't been for him I'd have never met Captain Dillon and had a purpose in life. And now he was gone.

I dropped to my knees beside him.

"Why did you do that?" I asked him. "Why did you have to be so brave?"

Not far away Danny Noyes lay dead. He and Bruce were two of my best friends in the unit and now they were both gone. They had shared their tent with us when we didn't have one. We'd shared meals and talked late into the night.

Captain Dillon walked over to us.

"Get up boys," he said.

We stood up.

"I know you must be hurting inside. We need to take their bodies down the hill now."

We stepped aside as some men loaded Bruce, Danny, and George onto stretchers and carried them off.

The three of us walked slowly down the hill. Crumb was very happy to see us. Preston took the rope off him and hugged him hard. I could see his shoulders shaking and knew he was crying into the dog's fur.

All around the camp, men stripped off their jackets and stood their rifles against each other. Everyone was very quiet.

Chapter 37

The three of us sat on a log by our tent. We didn't know for sure what to do. Captain Dillon and the other officers were gathered together talking lowly.

After a while they broke up and Captain Dillon came over by us. He squatted down by us.

"I know you boys were very close to Bruce and Lieutenant Noyse. I know this has to be very hard on you. But we have to move on boys. It's a terrible thing to lose a member of your unit in a war and even worse when that person is a friend, but the war goes on and the Sixth Wisconsin goes on too."

We nodded. Foster began crying.

Captain Dillon put his arm around him.

"Cry it out. There is no shame in crying."

He stood up.

"Our first need right now is a decent supper. The men are hungry and a good meal will lift their spirits. I've sent a couple of our officers to secure some better food from the town down the hill. When they get back will you three see to it that we have a good meal?"

"Yes Sir," I said.

"And tomorrow, we will say goodbye to our fallen men. I want to send them home with honor and want you three to make it memorable for the unit. Preston, do you know taps?"

"Yes Sir," he said.

"Eli and Foster, I want you to play a song fitting them as

they are taken off to the rail station."

"We'll do it Sir," I said.

He turned to leave. Then he turned back.

"I want you boys to take over the tent that Bruce and Danny had. Pack up their things in some boxes and move into that tent. There are three of you in that little dog tent and with that dog, it's got to be very crowded."

"Thank you Sir," Foster said.

He smiled at us. He didn't know that we'd been sharing Bruce and Danny's tent the whole time.

"I know this will live with you the rest of your lives, but be brave and remember these men as the valiant soldiers they were. Also remember them as some of the best friends you'll ever know."

We watched him walk off. Captain Dillon always walked tall and straight, almost marching. He was the picture of a military man, yet today he walked slowly, his head lowered and as if the weight of the world was on his shoulders.

It was hard to open the tent and sort through the personal things that had belonged to Bruce and Danny. We got a couple of crates from the carpenters. They were busy building five boxes to transport the bodies. We didn't linger there.

Once we had all of the personal stuff packed up, Preston and I carried it to the carpenters.

"It's going to feel strange in here without them," Foster said.

"They're here," I said, sitting in the tent with Bruce and Danny's stuff gone. "I hope they're watching over us."

Somehow, the officers came up with a dozen chickens, and a bunch of potatoes. One of them told me that they'd "liberated" the food from the rebels. A group of the men butchered and picked them and some others helped cut them up and the three of us mixed up some flour and spices and filled a big pot with oil to fry them in. We peeled the potatoes and boiled them in another big pot and to make sure we had enough food for everyone, we boiled some hardtack and then chopped it up and fried it too making it into crunchy little bread balls. It went well with the chicken and made the few chickens stretch enough that everyone had a full belly when we were done.

A bunch of the men pitched in to clean up and then everyone sat around campfires and talked quietly into the evening.

It had been a costly battle. In addition to the five men killed, we'd had twenty-one wounded. Our unit was one fourth of the strength it had been. Later that evening twenty-five men from the infantry joined our unit.

The three of us talked about what we'd do in the morning when they came to take the bodies away. We'd talked to one of the lieutenants and he said there were two wagons coming. Danny and Bruce would be in one and the other three would be in the other, in their caskets. They'd be taken through the camp and then onto the road to town where they'd be loaded onto a train and taken back to Richland County.

"How far is it?" Preston asked.

"I don't know Preston," I said. "It's a long way. A long, long way."

We settled down in our tent. It was much roomier for us but all of us would have been happy to be crowded like before if we could have Bruce and Danny back.

After a breakfast of oatmeal, the officers called the unit to order and had them line the track through the camp where the wagons would go. The two wagons pulled up to the end of the line and stopped with the five caskets in the back.

Captain Dillon stepped out in the middle of the road.

"Men, today we say farewell to five of our brave soldiers.

You all knew them and you fought beside them. They were brothers to some, sons to others, and friends to all. They died bravely in the service of their country and to save the Union. Please stand at attention and salute them as they pass."

He nodded at Preston. I could see his hand shaking as he lifted his bugle. The first notes of taps rang through the valley. Tears ran down my face as he played the mournful song. When he was finished, he stood at attention and I began a drum roll. The wagons began moving slowly down the road between our men. They all saluted as they passed.

Foster began playing the *Battle Hymn of the Republic*. Many sang along with it. I kept beating the drum roll and Foster played until the wagons cleared the crest of the hill and were gone from sight. We finished and the men were dismissed.

The three of us stood there. We'd all been crying. I felt like I was hollow inside.

Chapter 38

The twenty-five infantry men and our remaining uninjured men joined up with the other units at Corinth and set out pursuing the enemy south for the next week. My friends and I and the wounded stayed in camp with the doctors and the men who took care of the horses. We weren't sure if it was safe to go out fishing or foraging so we stayed in camp that week. When Captain Dillon and the unit returned we were told that we would stay on duty where we were until the Generals let us know where we'd go next.

"We should go fishing," Preston said.

I asked Captain Dillon if it was safe for us to go out fishing or foraging and he said he thought all of the rebels were long gone. So we decided to get out of camp for a while.

We got our hooks and lines and took Crumb along with us. We knew there was a river in the valley so we headed that way. Usually we laughed and talked and fooled around on the way fishing but today we just walked along quietly.

We came to a woods and split up to look for worms. We turned over logs and picked up fishing worms and grubs and put them in a coffee cup. When we had enough to fish for a while we walked along until we came to the river. It wasn't a real big river but looked like it probably had some fish in it.

Foster took his pocketknife and cut three willow branches and stripped off the leaves and side branches. We each took one and tied a line on it with a hook and sinker. Then we sat on the bank and put our lines in the water.

"It's going to be different," I said.

They both nodded.

"I can't believe both Danny and Bruce died," Preston said, his voice shaking.

"It's a war Preston," I said. "We've been lucky so far that they were the first ones to die. We've had some die of diseases but you know what we heard about some of those battles where hundreds died. We're lucky we weren't in a battle like that."

"When we started all of this, everyone said the war would be over in a few months. The rebels didn't have any industry and the north had all of the guns and stuff. We've been at it now for a year and it doesn't look like we're anywhere close to the end," Foster said.

I caught a catfish. I put it on a string and in the water.

"I wonder how far it is to get home?" Preston asked.

We caught a fish now and then and after a while Preston put his fishing pole on the bank.

"I'm going for a walk," he said.

He got up and walked off toward the hill.

"I wonder where he's going?" Foster asked.

"He's really homesick. Even though he's got his brothers here, he misses his mom and dad," I said.

"We all miss our friends and families," Foster added.

I had no family to miss. The closest thing I had to a family was Bruce and now he was gone. There was one person I did miss. I thought of Kathy Jane and her golden hair and her smile and blue eyes. I wished I could hold her and tell her how I missed her.

Preston didn't come back and we began getting worried.

"What if he ran into some stray rebels and got captured?"

"There shouldn't be any rebels this far north."

Half an hour later he still wasn't back.

"We should go look for him," I said.

We pulled up our poles. We'd seen where he headed and followed that way. He'd gone up the hill so we climbed up and looked around for him. Crumb sniffed along and seemed to be following his trail.

"Do you think Crumb smells him?"

"I thought all he smelled was food. Maybe he can smell him," I said.

"Hey Crumb, go find Preston."

The dog's tail wagged and he set out and seemed to be following a trail of some kind."

"He probably smells a deer or something," Foster said.

We followed the dog up the hill and soon we came to a stand of huge pine trees. Crumb sniffed around and then looked up into a really tall tree and began barking. We walked next to the tree and looked up. Way up in the top we could see Preston sitting on a branch.

"Holy smokes, he's up there!" I said.

"Hey Preston, what the heck are you doing?"

He looked down. "I'll be down in a minute," he said.

We waited while he climbed down from the tree. He got to the lower branch and jumped the rest of the way.

"What the heck were you doing up there?" I asked.

"I thought if I got way up there, I might be able to see home."

Foster looked at me.

"Home is a long way off Preston. There's no way you can see it from here."

"I just thought. I thought maybe I'd see our valley and our windmill. I know it sounds crazy but I hoped I might see my Ma."

His eyes filled with tears. I put my arm on his shoulder.

"They're home waiting for us to come back," I said. "We signed up to do a job and when we've done it we'll come home and be heroes."

"We ain't done nothing much to be heroes," he said.

"Everyone has his part to do. Maybe we just play music and cook, but that's part of it."

"We'll always have this as something to talk about for the rest of our lives," Foster said.

He stood there and wiped his eyes.

"Why do you think Bruce did that? I mean what made him charge that officer like that?"

"I think he was so brave that he didn't think about anything but stopping that man from claiming our unit. He was named Leonidas after the Spartan king and his 300 men who stood against thousands and fought to the last man. He told me once that he was destined to be a brave warrior."

"He was brave, that's for sure."

"I wish he'd not been so brave and we'd still have him here with us."

"We'll always have our time with him to remember him," I said.

We walked back to the river and fished until late afternoon. We had a pretty good string of fish and that night everyone had a good supper. It seemed strange seeing that our dog tent was gone and that we now had the bigger tent.

I lay there with Crumb nestled up next to me and thought of the nights we'd spent in this tent with Bruce and Danny and the stories they told and how we laughed at some of the things Bruce told us.

I thought about how Bruce had teased me about my "girlfriend". I decided I should write a letter to Kathy Jane in the morning.

Chapter 39

Dear Kathy Jane,

Today I write with a heavy heart. You may already know that Bruce and Lieutenant Danny Noyse and three other of our men were killed in the battle of Corinth on the 4th day of October. This was the first time I really knew that we were in a real war and had a chance of dying. Up until that day we'd had some men die of sickness but to have them die in battle really made it clear that there is much danger.

I don't mean to frighten you. Preston, Foster and I are always back away from where the most danger is, so we're pretty safe. So please don't worry about me.

The weather is cooling off and it's much nicer here now. We don't know where we'll be going next but I'll send you a letter when we get there. I can imagine Lone Rock now, with the leaves falling and the squirrels running through the trees. I always loved fall and hunting and the cool temperatures. I miss that, and of course I miss you too.

I think of you every day. I can barely wait until the day we come home so I can see you again.

Yours,
Eli

We broke camp and left Corinth on November 2nd. We marched through Grand Junction, Davis' Mills, and LaGrange, to Moscow, Tennessee. There we joined up with General

Grant's army and passed through Holly Springs and camped at Lumpkins' Mills. From there we followed pursuit of the enemy who had evacuated Tallahassee and were retreating south. We went as far as the Yocona River, south of Oxford, Mississippi and were involved in the sacking of Holly Springs where we were split into two units, one under Lieutenant Clark. His half of the unit was sent to Memphis as an escort to a supply train, while the rest of the unit returned to Holly Springs and later to LaFayette, Tennessee where we rejoined Lieutenant Clark.

On January 2nd, 1863, we went into winter quarters at Buntyn's Station five miles east of Memphis. We'd marched hundreds of miles in the two months after Corinth and it sounded like a good thing go make a camp that we'd stay in for a while.

All the time on the march had been hard on the men and the horses. Everyone needed some rest and some better food. We were all sick and tired of hardtack and salt pork, so as soon as we got settled, we set out foraging and looking for a place to fish.

Tennessee was really nice now that it was winter. The temperature was perfect and there was a nice river nearby and lots of woods for hunting. Many of the big homes were deserted but there were a few crops in the fields that had been left behind.

Our men foraged and the three of us fished and hunted squirrels and rabbits. We had pretty good chow most of the time.

I realized one day that I had turned 16 a week earlier. I didn't bother to tell anyone. For some reason a birthday didn't seem very important.

I got a letter from Kathy Jane.

My Dearest Eli,
The winter is upon us here. You know how cold it can get in January. I imagine it must be a lot warmer there in the south.
There were many people gathered when the bodies of our brave men were brought home. The people of the town and the area treated them like the hero's they were. Bruce was buried in Button Cemetery and Danny Noyse was buried in Sac Prairie Cemetery. It was very sad to see his widow and his small child.
I say a prayer every night for you and your safety. I don't know what I'd do if something happened to you. You mean so much to me Eli.
I got that last money you sent home. It's all safe and sound and waiting for you when you return. I expect you'll have something in mind to do with it.
Be safe and be well my sweet Eli. You are in my thoughts every minute of the day.

With love,
Kathy Jane

I read the letter and saw that she said she sent love to me. I hadn't thought about it that way but once she'd said that I realized I loved her too. Somehow she'd changed from a girl who was kind of pest to a young woman who was in my thoughts a lot. It was a bit frightening to think about being in love, but it wasn't so bad as I thought it might be.

Chapter 40

We were excited about moving on and on March 1st we left Memphis and headed downriver to Grand Lake, Arkansas. We didn't stay there but a few hours and turned around and camped on a sand bar opposite the head of the Yazoo pass, four miles below Helena. Then we joined the Yazoo pass expedition moving down the pass on transports as far as Greenwood. We were under the command of Lieutenant Clark and moved against the rebel fortifications from then to the middle of April. By May 1st we were a part of the battle of Thompson's Hill.

We were put in a position to prevent a flank movement and on the 2nd we pursued the retreating enemy, until we were stopped by a burning bridge that the rebels had set afire over the Black River.

We were exhausted and worn out but the war went on. We had taken two wounded at Jackson on the 14th. It didn't matter that we were tired and hungry. We left Jackson the next morning and by the 16th we were engaged in a hotly fought contest at Champion Hills. We had two more men wounded at that battle.

We musicians helped with the wounded as much as we could. For a long time we'd had few wounded and the medical people could keep up with them. Most of the ones being taken care of were sick with dysentery or the "loose ladies" diseases.

But now there were many wounded and there was a lot of

work to do to help them. We did what we could, keeping them fed and washed. Some had lost legs or arms and it was pretty hard to see that for the first few times we helped but we soon got used to it.

Our new friend Henry Ashby had gotten his eyes burned with a powder flash in the last battle and was in the hospital resting. We sat and talked with him to keep him company.

He told us that he had been born a slave in Missouri in 1832. He didn't know for sure what his birth date was because slaves were more like cattle than people to the southern plantation owners. When the civil war broke out he ran away and went north. He found the engineer company and they took him in and then he met Lt. Clark and was brought into our unit.

"You sure can go up and down hills fast," Foster said.

Henry smiled.

"You learn to work fast and hard when you're a slave. I guess I just learned to do things like that and now it's hard not to.

"I wish we had a lot more like you Henry," I said. "We'd win this war in no time."

On the 19th we took up positions around the fortifications at Vicksburg. We opened fire and were actively engaged every day during the siege. The men were exhausted. When Vicksburg surrendered, we had seven more wounded and another of our men killed. Alva Page was shot in the left ear by a sniper under a flag of truce. He died before he hit the ground. The sniper was hunted down and killed also. The hospital tent was bulging with injured men.

We were told that we'd be there for a while so the three of us went looking for something to eat that wasn't hard tack or salt pork. We took a rifle along with us just in case.

We were walking along a dirt road toward a valley that we figured would have some kind of a stream in it. We hoped to find a place to fish. Crumb was galloping around having a lot of fun. He'd grown up now and was a big dog. Preston suggested we stop calling him Crumb and call him Loaf, but we didn't think that was a good idea.

"We could borrow a saddle and ride him," Preston offered.

We laughed about that one but it was almost true.

We came over a rise and there was a big house. The weeds were grown up around it and the front door was hanging open on one hinge. There was a fence on the side yard that looked like it may have enclosed a garden at one time.

"Let's see if there's anything there," I said.

Crumb was ahead of us and he ran into the house. Suddenly there was a lot of hollering and a black man came running out the front door. Behind him were three little kids and a woman. They were terrified of Crumb. Then they saw us in our Union uniforms and carrying a gun and they really were scared.

They all stopped and put their hands in the air. The kids, two boys and a girl were all crying except for the older boy.

"Don shoot us please. We not rebels."

Foster put the gun down by his side. Crumb came up to them wagging his tail.

"He won't hurt you," I said.

"He came after us."

"He was just looking around. He's just a pup."

"Pup? Heck that dog is big as a pony."

"He's friendly," Preston said.

The older boy put his hand out and Crumb sniffed it and then licked it. He smiled.

"He's okay Pap."

"Why don't you put your hands down? We're not going to

hurt you," I said.

"Ya'll are soldiers yeah?"

"We're musicians. We play the drum and fife and bugle."

They looked confused.

"Ya'll got a band in the army?"

We laughed.

"We play the calls to tell the men what to do, like when to fire the artillery," I said.

"So ya'lls not huntin' rebels?"

"We're hunting something to eat."

The father looked at his wife and she nodded.

"Might know where they's some stuff," he said.

"We won't take it all. You have to eat too. But if you could help us out we'd be mighty obliged."

Foster was carrying our fishing poles and our little jar of hooks and lines. The older boy looked at them.

"Ya'll fish?"

"We were looking for a place to fish. You know any?"

"Uh huh. Don't got no hooks though."

"We've got hooks. You show us a spot to fish and we'll share with you."

The kid looked at his dad. They both smiled.

"Deal," the kid said.

Chapter 41

We found out that the father's name was Abraham, the older boy was Jonah and the little guy was Isaac. The little girl was Mary and the mom was Helen. They had been the slaves of a family that lived in the house and owned the farm. When the war came to them, the owners left and told the family to stay behind and take care of the place.

"We don't got no money but we got a little food hid."

"They just left you behind?" I asked.

"They said they got no room for us," Jonah replied. "Don't think they too worried if we get killed or not."

"You know, President Lincoln freed all of the slaves," Foster said.

"What you say? Who be President Lincoln?"

We explained to them and they were surprised to hear that they were now free.

"Don't think we better act free until we sure," Abraham said. "We just goin be stayin out of sight mostly and wait to see what happens."

"Well how about that fishing spot?" Preston asked.

The two boys went with us and the parents and the little girl stayed at the house. Jonah led us to a river and then to his secret spot. It was where there was a bend in the river and there was a nice bank to sit on and fish. We cut two new poles out of willows for the two of them and rigged them up with hooks and lines.

Then we hunted for some grubs and worms and when we had some we sat down and began fishing.

"Ya'll get paid to play that music?" Isaac asked us.

"We do. We're supposed to get thirteen dollars a month but some months go by and we don't get paid. We hope that it will catch up one of these months."

"Thirteen dollars? Holy smokes that much?"

"Yeah, it's not bad pay and we get our food and uniforms free."

"Wow, we should sign up for that Jonah," the little guy said.

"Don't spose they have black soldiers," he said.

"We have one black man. He ran away from his owners when the war started and now he's a member of our unit," I said.

"I think there are some black units," Preston said. "I've heard of them."

They shook their heads in wonder.

"When the war is over you should be able to get jobs and get paid too," Foster said to them. They acted like that was never going to happen.

We fished for a while and caught some fish. We moved to another spot and caught a bunch more. It wasn't long and we had a nice bunch of them.

"We should start back," I said.

"We got some pails at the house. We could get a couple for ya'll to carry the fish."

That sounded like a good idea. We walked back and talked along the way. These boys were just like us, except somebody owned them. That was kind of hard to understand.

When we got back we took part of the fish and left them with part. Abraham led us to a little shed off in the distance. It looked like it was going to fall down but he opened a door and went in and lifted up a section of the floor. There were some baskets and pails down in a hole in the ground that held potatoes and carrots and some big red and yellow things that we'd never seen before.

"What's that?" I asked.

Abraham handed me one of the balls. It was heavy and hard as a rock.

"That be a rutabaga."

"You eat it?"

"Heck yeah. They pretty hard but you cook them like a tater. Good for ya'll."

We ended up with a pail with some potatoes, carrots, two onions and half a dozen rutabagas. We had a good load of food for the camp.

"It was fun fishing with you," Preston said to Jonah and Isaac.

"Heck yeah. Thanks for sharing the fish."

"You keep those hooks and then you can fish some more."

We handed them four more hooks so they'd have some spares.

Abraham thanked us and we shook hands with him. He seemed surprised that we'd do that.

"What's wrong?" Foster asked.

"Ya'll treat us like we's people like you."

That seemed funny. They were people like us. They looked a little different and talked a little different but they were just like us otherwise.

"Where we come from, people treat other people kindly," I said.

"Where is it that ya'll come from?"

"They call it Wisconsin."

"Must be a nice place."

We all smiled.

"It's a heck of a nice place. If you ever get up north, come and look for us in Lone Rock in Wisconsin."

They said they would.

We headed back to camp with a whole bunch of fish, a nice pail full of potatoes, carrots, onions and something called rutabagas. It'd been a good day.

Chapter 42

The weather was hot again but it was nearly the end of August so we knew it would soon cool off some. We'd been in camp near Vicksburg for a while and the men had taken the time to rest up and get their gear in order for our next deployment.

We'd found several good fishing spots and the men had gone foraging and had come back with a lot of good stuff to add to the meals we were cooking.

Preston was very popular in the camp and was pretty proud of all the praise he got for taking some common things and turning them into some pretty darn good meals.

"I might open a restaurant when I get home," he said one day, as he and I were cleaning fish.

"You think you could make a living doing that?"

"I think so, if I made good food."

"But most people eat at home, and the mother makes the food."

"My Ma's a horrible cook," Foster said.

"Really?" I asked laughing.

"She can't cook for sour apples. My Pa does most of the cooking."

"Hmm, well maybe a restaurant would be something," I said. "There is a little place in Lone Rock that has food. I never ate there, cause I never had any money."

"Well maybe I'll start another place and you can come and spend money with me," Preston said.

"As good as you cook, I'd come every day."
"How bout you Eli? What are you going to do?"
"He's going to marry Kathy Jane," Foster said giggling.
I threw a fish at him.

On September 12th we loaded up on transports and headed up river, disembarking at Helena on the 15th. From there we marched to Little Rock and re-enforced General Steel. Later we moved up to Memphis and then in October we reported to General Sherman at Glendale, Mississippi. From there we spent time in Iuka, Mississippi, Florence, Alabama and Winchester, Tennessee. We arrived in Chattanooga on the 20th of November.

We'd moved a lot in two months and hadn't been at one place long enough to do much fishing or foraging so we'd been living on hard tack and salt pork pretty much the whole while. We were hoping to have a little time in Chattanooga but four days later we crossed the river with Sherman's forces and one of our gun sections was stationed at Mission Ridge, having had the guns drawn up to the top by ropes. We engaged in the battle of Mission Ridge and then joined the 26th and pursued the rebels into Georgia and finally returned back to Chattanooga were our guns were turned over to the ordinance officers. They condemned the guns as worn out.

We left Chattanooga on December 2nd and returned to Bridgeport where we remained in camp until the 22nd. This gave us some time to organize some foraging groups and soon Preston was cooking up some fine meals. We were hoping to remain there for a while but on the 22nd, we left and moved to Larkinville, Alabama. We arrived the day after Christmas and stayed until January 7, 1864. Then we marched to Huntsville where we went into winter quarters and were equipped with a new battery of 12-pound Napoleon guns.

I turned 17 while we were in Huntsville and wouldn't have even thought about it except that I got a letter from Kathy Jane on my birthday.

My Dearest Eli,

I hope this letter gets to you by your birthday and I hope you had a wonderful celebration. I wish I could have been with you to give you a special gift. I'll keep it for you until you get home.

There is talk that the South is faltering and that the war will not go on much longer. I pray every day that this is true and that soon you and all of the others will be home safe.

Have you thought of what you'll do when you get home? My mother is getting to the age where she thinks she cannot take care of the store any longer and is hinting that I should take it over. I'm not sure about it but it would be something to think about. I know you still have your family farm and expect that you'd like to live there. I've thought of living in the country many times and would love to see it when you get home.

I will close now and please be sure that I think of you every day and pray for you. I miss you terribly Eli. I can't wait until we are able to be together again.

Love.
Kathy Jane

Holy smokes. I hadn't thought of what I'd do when I got home. I guess that I'd have to do something more than live in Captain Dillon's tailor shop. The idea of Kathy Jane taking over the general store sounded like a good one. It seemed that she was hinting that maybe I'd like to help her with it. I wasn't sure about that but it sure was something to think about.

Chapter 43

That night in our tent the three of us lay talking.

"I see you got a letter from your girlfriend," Foster said.

"I keep telling you we're friends," I said.

"What do you think she looks like now?" Preston asked.

"What do you mean?"

"Eli, we've been gone two years. Look at us, you're half a foot taller, I'm not that much taller but a bit and Foster has grown almost a foot. Kathy Jane surely has grown taller and probably more... curvy."

He grinned at me.

"You think?" I asked.

"She was pretty cute when we left. If she got more womanly, she is probably a good-looking woman now."

"She's probably too pretty for old Eli," Foster said. "He wouldn't know what to do with all those womanly curves."

"Oh? How do you know so much? Have you ever kissed a girl Foster?"

"Heck yeah."

"Who?"

Foster turned red.

"Who Foster," Preston asked.

"My Ma."

We laughed and laughed. I looked at Preston.

"How about you?"

He blushed too.

"Did you kiss your Ma too?"

"Yeah, but somebody else too."

"Who!?"

Foster and I were pretty excited.

"You know Gertie Manning?"

I knew Gertie Manning. She was a farm girl from the area where Preston lived.

"I think I know her," I said.

"What does she look like?" Foster asked.

"Well she's got nice dark hair that she wears in pigtails," I said. "And she's got blue eyes, and is um..."

"Go ahead and say it," Preston said. "She's a little on the husky side."

Foster burst out laughing.

"Husky?"

"She's big boned," Preston said. "But boy can she cook. She taught me a lot of the stuff I know about cooking."

"So you kissed her?" I asked.

Preston grinned.

"Heck yeah. I kissed her lots of times."

We talked late into the night and the more we talked about home, the more I longed to be there again. When we left Lone Rock we thought that the war was near the end already. The thought was that it would be over by the following spring. That seemed like a long time ago.

We'd come many miles and seen many things, some horrible. The idea of a simple steady life in the Wisconsin River valley looked pretty appealing to us.

That night I dreamt of Kathy Jane. In my dream we were walking along the river in the wet sand, barefoot, holding hands. When I woke the next morning, I wrote a letter to her.

Dear Kathy Jane,

I got your letter on my birthday. Thanks for sending it or I might have forgotten that I turned seventeen. Wow, it's kind of scary being this old. The time has passed quickly here. I can't imagine how things have changed there. I can't wait to see you and spend time together talking about everything that has happened to both of us during my absence.

I think the idea of running the general store is a good one. I think I could help out now and then if you needed someone to help. I've thought about the farm and that might be something too. I own the land and the cabin now, so I think I'd like to fix it up and try a little farming. I guess we'll have to talk about it together.

Do you think you'd like to live in the country? I like it out there. The house isn't very fancy but it could be fixed up and added to. I have a pretty good bit of money I think and I could use that to add to the house. I'd also like to build a little barn for a few cows and maybe have some chickens. But that's all a long way off. We have to get his war over so we can go on with our lives.

We're on railroad guard duty now and will probably be here until spring. Then I have no idea where we will go. I've seen enough of the south. I long to see the hills of Wisconsin and the green valleys along the River... and of course, you.

Love,
Eli

I hesitated when I wrote the word love, but Kathy Jane used it so I guessed it was okay for me to use it too. I wasn't sure if I was doing the right thing but it seemed right.

On November 10th we left for Nashville and joined the reserve battery at Fort Barry. We spent the rest of the fall there and on January 7, 1865 we were transferred to the reserve garrison. Our men were armed with muskets on January 16, and assigned to guard duty. The war was winding down.

Chapter 44

There was a lot of talk among the men about the end of the war coming soon. We heard of battles where the south lost badly and it seemed they were in retreat all the time.

Every now and then a group of soldiers from another unit were transferred to our unit. Many of them were from units that had lost several men. They were always welcomed and we all tried to do our best to stay busy, even though all we had was guard duty.

Preston, Foster and I organized some of the men into foraging units and with their finds and other fishing and hunting we had some pretty good food. The entire camp looked forward to those days when the foraging had been good. Captain Dillon was very proud of us, and the things we, well Preston, could do with the stuff we had to work with.

One morning about the middle of January, a small group of soldiers came into the camp led by a lieutenant. He asked around and soon came to Captain Dillon's tent. We were outside of our tent around a campfire when he walked up. He looked pretty bedraggled.

"Can you tell me where to find Captain Dillon?" he asked.

I got up and went to the Captain's tent and told him he had a visitor. Captain Dillon came out and invited the young officer into this tent. Some time later they came out and Captain Dillon came over to us.

"This young man has twenty-one men with him. He also

has a musician and I'd like you boys to show them to an area and have our men help them get some tents up and make them comfortable. They've had a tough time and they are pretty worn out."

We were happy to have something to do.

"Happy to Sir," I said.

"And I was wondering, since you have a large tent, would you mind letting the musician stay with you?"

"No problem Captain," Preston said.

We followed the lieutenant to the group of men. They looked pretty sad. Many of them had bad limps and they were very thin and pale. It was obvious they'd been in many battles because a lot of them had bandages on their arms or legs. We found a boy a little younger than us and figured he was the musician.

"Hey," I said as I walked up to him.

"Hey yourself."

"We're musicians and Captain Dillon asked if you'd like to stay with us. We've got a larger tent and we'd be happy to have you."

"I guess," he said.

"What's your name?"

"Tommy."

"I'm Eli, this is Preston and that's Foster."

He nodded to us.

"There aren't many of you in your unit," Preston said.

He shook his head sadly. His eyes filled with tears.

"They just about killed us all," he said.

We stood there not knowing what to do or say. Finally Preston asked him if he was hungry. It was pretty obvious he hadn't been eating much.

"I been hungry for three weeks," he said.

"Come on, our men will help your guys, and you come with us. We're kind of the unofficial camp cooks. We'll get you something to chew on."

He walked to the other men and told them he'd be staying with us. Then the four of us went to our tent. When he saw Crumb lying in the opening of the tent he stopped short.

"Holy smokes, is that dog mean?"

"No he's real friendly," I said. "Come here Crumb."

Crumb got up and walked to Tommy and wagged his tail. The kid rubbed Crumb's ears and Crumb licked his hand.

"Crumb?"

I laughed.

"When we got him he was just a little thing, like a crumb."

"Looks like a pony now," Tommy said.

"He eats like one too."

Preston went to the kitchen and came back with a couple of biscuits with some jam on them and a piece of cheese.

"This isn't much but we're going fishing today and we'll have a good supper," he said as he handed Tommy the food. His eyes got big and he ate like he was famished. It only took him a couple of minutes and he had the food gone.

"Where did you get those biscuits? I haven't had a biscuit like that since I left Green Bay."

"Preston makes them," I said.

"He's a magician with food," Foster added. "You live in Green Bay?"

"That's where I came from. If I make it back to Wisconsin, that's where I'll go."

"We're from Lone Rock. I bet you've never heard of it."

"Can't rightly say I have, where is it by?"

"It's west of Madison."

He shrugged.

"The war is nearly over. You'll be home in no time," I said.

"I hope so. After Gettysburg and several battles after it, I didn't think I'd live this long."

"You were at Gettysburg?"

He nodded and I could tell he didn't want to talk about it.

"What instrument do you play?" Foster asked.

"Drum."

"Me too," I said.

"Let's get your stuff in the tent," Preston suggested.

Tommy didn't have much. His blanket was worn and very dirty. His uniform was filthy and the legs of his pants were stained with a dark blackish stain. His shoes were also covered with whatever was on his pants.

"We should wash your stuff," I said.

"I got no other clothes to wear," he said.

"We need to wash ours too. Let's take our fishing stuff and we can wash first and then we'll fish. There are a bunch of guys going fishing today and some others looking for potatoes and stuff. We're going to have a feast tonight if the fish bite."

"You know how to fish?" Foster asked.

"Heck yeah."

We got our fishing gear and some soap and headed to the river. Even though it was January, it was warm enough to wash our clothes and take a bath in the river. At first Tommy looked surprised when we stripped our clothes off but soon he joined us. We waded into the river and washed the clothes.

"What's that on your pants?" Preston asked.

"It's blood."

"Really?"

Tommy nodded sadly.

"I don't want to talk about it right now," he said.

We finished washing the clothes and took them and hung them on branches to dry. The sun was shining and there was a nice breeze so it wouldn't take long. We washed ourselves in the river and then got out and sat on the grass to dry off.

"What if a rebel came along and caught you all naked?"

Tommy asked.

"We haven't seen a rebel around here for a while. Anyway if he saw a bunch of naked guys, he'd probably run the other way."

Tommy laughed at that. It was the first time we'd seen him smile.

An hour later everything was dry and we dressed and went down the river a little way and off into the river bottoms to a good fishing spot we'd found a week earlier. We stopped in the woods and rolled over logs and picked up a bunch of worms for bait. Then we sat side-by-side on the bank and put our lines out.

It didn't take long and Preston caught a nice crappie. We'd brought a piece of twine and slid it through his gills and tied it and then put him in the pond and tied the string to a branch. We'd hardly gotten him in the water when Tommy caught a bluegill.

From then on we caught fish one after another.

Chapter 45

We ended up with a lot of fish. Tommy had the biggest one when he caught a really big bass. We carried the fish back to camp and met with some of the others who were already cleaning the fish they'd caught. We joined in and it took nearly an hour to clean them all.

"Oh boy we're going to have a feast tonight," Foster said.

The men who'd been out foraging came back with a few potatoes, some carrots and some rutabagas.

"What's these things?" Tommy asked as he hefted a rutabaga.

"They call them rutabagas," I said. "They're hard as a rock but if you cut them up in small chunks and boil them they taste kind of like spicy potatoes. We mix them right in with the taters."

Tommy helped us peel them and cut them up and we put them in a couple of pots to boil. Then we got a bunch of frying pans and began frying fish. It didn't take long for the men to line up to eat.

We kept frying fish while everyone ate and when they were finished we fried the last of the fish and sat down to eat too. Tommy ate like he'd been starving for a long time.

"This is the first fish I've had since I left home. Back in Green Bay I went down to the lake almost every day and caught fish. I sure miss that."

"We all miss home," I said.

"Were you three friends before?"

"Preston and I knew each other but not well. Actually his name is Oscar but he goes by Preston. Foster is from another town where our other captain is from."

Tommy looked at Preston.

"Oscar?"

"The man who taught me to play the bugle was also a musician in the Spanish American War. His best friend was named Preston. He was killed, so I took that name to honor him."

Tommy's eyes filled with tears. He turned away.

Preston put his hand on Tommy's shoulder.

"Did I say something wrong?"

Tommy shook his head.

"I joined with two of my friends. They're both dead."

The three of us were stunned. We'd been touched by death with the loss of Bruce and Danny and the others that had died but it never had entered our minds that one of us might have been killed.

"Sorry, we didn't know," I said.

"It's okay," Tommy said. "I wish you guys could have known them. They were great friends."

"Please tell us about them," Foster said.

Tommy took a deep breath and began his story: "The three of us grew up on the same street. I was the youngest, David was a little older than me and Terrence was the oldest. He was about a year older than me. We became friends when we were just little guys and we lived close to Lake Michigan so we fished almost every day. When the talk of war started we talked about it and what an adventure it would be. The more we talked about it, the more it seemed like the thing to do, so we went to a place where they were signing up people to be soldiers.

"I was only eleven, David had just turned twelve and

Terrence was almost thirteen, but they said we were too young. They asked us if we played any instruments. Of course none of us did but we said we'd learn. So I guess it was probably like you guys, they found a man to teach us and I became the drummer, David played the flife and Terrence played the bugle.

"We were very excited when we got uniforms and our own tent and the next thing we were on a train going to the south. Our unit was infantry and the first battle we were in, we lost three men and had six wounded. Our officers had us help carrying the killed and wounded from the field of battle on stretchers. It was a real awakening to see men with blood pouring from them and missing legs and arms."

"We had the same thing," I said. "It made the war very real."

Tommy nodded.

"Over the next year we were in many battles and then we were at Gettysburg. We had no idea it would be anything different than what we'd been through in other battles. But it was the battle of Gettysburg that changed everything.

"It started on the first day of July, 1863 and went on for the next two days. Our unit was made up of one hundred and sixteen enlisted men, six officers and the three of us. When the battle was over, thirty-seven of our men were dead, nearly fifty were wounded and fourteen were missing and probably had been taken prisoner. Two of our officers were killed and... David was dead."

"Oh no," Preston said.

"We were right by the officers like always, so we could send messages by drum and bugle and David was right next to me. The rebels were hidden in the trees and they had snipers and one second David was talking to me, and the next he was laying on the ground with a bullet through his throat.

"Terrence and I tried to help him but there was nothing

we could do. He died in less than a minute."

We all were stunned. We'd not even considered that one of us might have died like that.

"Afterward, it took a week to get all of the killed taken care of and the wounded patched up. Several of the wounded were hurt badly enough that they couldn't keep fighting and were shipped home. The rest rested up and soon most were ready to get back into the fight. Then we went to another battle, and another and another. A couple of weeks ago we were supporting an artillery unit in Georgia. Terrence and I were next to the officers like we always were. The rebels were firing their big guns into our ranks. Terrence was three feet from me. He turned to say something and suddenly he dropped to the ground. I looked down..."

Tommy stopped and bent over to catch his breath.

"Terrence's legs were gone. A cannon ball had hit him just above the knees and cut him down. I dropped to the ground and held him in my arms and tried to comfort him. He knew he was going to die. He told me to think of him when I got back to Green Bay and went fishing in our old spots. He died in my arms."

No one said a word. There was nothing we could say.

"That was his blood that was all over my uniform," Tommy said. "There were only a handful of us left so we were assigned to support your unit here."

Foster got up and hugged Tommy. Then Preston and I did the same. We didn't know what else to do.

"I think it's time for some sleep," I said.

We crawled into the tent with Crumb and bedded down.

"Thank you for sharing that with us Tommy," I said. "I know it must have been hard."

"It was but I needed to talk about it. Now it's time to move   on."

Chapter 46

For the next few weeks we spent a lot of time fishing and foraging. There wasn't much else to do. Tommy began to be more talkative and looked a lot better after he had some good meals and was away from the fighting.

There were all kinds of rumors about the end of the war but no one really knew anything for sure. On February 17th we broke camp and marched to Chattanooga to a permanent camp. The word was that when the war ended we'd go home from there. We were very excited about the idea of going home but little did we know that it would take five more months for that to happen.

My eighteenth birthday came and went without much notice. For some reason a birthday seemed pretty insignificant. The three of us had all grown from skinny kids to young men in the time we'd spent in the army. Looking at my two best friends I marveled at how much we'd changed.

Foster had grown very tall and had filled out to be a big strapping guy. He had a few whiskers on his chin and had let his red hair grow out so he looked like a big tough Irishman. We knew he wasn't very tough though.

Preston had also grown quite tall. He was still skinny but had that smile on his face all the time. He never seemed to be sad and his bright blue eyes sparkled when he told stories or when we fished and he caught a big one.

All three of us had gotten larger uniforms. The pants had

been way too short and the jackets and shirts were too small for all of us. They had two pair of longer pants so Preston and Foster took them since they'd grown more than I had. Our shoes had gotten too small too and when we got new ones, we learned that they'd come from others who had been killed. It was a little strange putting on someone else's shoes, especially someone who had been killed, but we couldn't run about barefoot, so we wore the shoes and we glad to get them.

Word reached Captain Dillon that General Robert E. Lee, surrendered his army to Union General Ulysses S. Grant at Appomatox Court House on April 9th. There was much rejoicing and we sang and fired off rounds into the air late into the night.

On April 16, news spread through the camp that President Lincoln had been assassinated on the 14th of that month. Everyone was very sad to hear the news.

We expected to get the orders to leave for home any day but soon we found that it was going to take longer than we expected. It seemed that everything the army did took a long time and we'd just have to wait.

About the middle of June the four of us set out to go fishing. We decided to try some new places since the fishing was getting slow at our old spots. We took two horses and rode bareback with two of us on each horse. About half a mile from the river there was a hillside that was very thick with brush. I noticed Preston looking hard at the brush and he steered his horse over near it.

"Holy smokes," he hollered.

"What's wrong?"

"There's berries here. There's millions of them!"

We all jumped off the horses and ran to the berry patch. The patch was huge and the bushes were covered with blackberries. We began picking them and eating them. Half an hour later we all were full of berries and hadn't made a dent in the patch.

"We need some buckets," I said.

"It's so far back to camp though," Foster said.

"But we should pick a bunch and take them back. Just imagine how the happy the men would be. We can eat them fresh and make pies and all kinds of stuff," Preston added.

"I'll go," Tommy said. "I'm a good rider."

"Get all the buckets and cloth bags you can find," I said." Tommy jumped up on one of the horses and away he went.

"We can't just sit here," Foster said.

"Let's take off our shirts and fill them with berries," I suggested.

Soon we were in the patch and each of us had laid his shirt on the ground. We picked berries and put them in our shirts until the shirts were piled with them. Then we picked up the corners and carried them out of the patch. We were trying to figure out how to keep picking when we heard a clatter and saw Tommy riding back with a bunch of pails tied on a rope on the back of his horse.

He rode up and we took the pails and began picking again. It was a glorious afternoon and we picked many buckets of berries. We dumped the ones from our shirts into some buckets and when we had all of the buckets full we decided to head back to camp. The ride back was pretty slow. Each horse had two guys on his back and four or five buckets of berries. Our hands were blue from all the berry juice and our faces were pretty blue too.

Captain Dillon was standing near his tent when we rode in. He looked at us and then grinned.

"It looks like you boys have been busy," he said.

"Yes Sir," I said. "We're having blackberries tonight."

"So you missed the news."

We all four stopped.

"What news Captain?"

"We've been ordered to clean all of our guns and other gear, take a census of all ordinance and equipment and report to the train station in two weeks."

We stood there waiting.

"Where are we going Sir?"

"Home boys. We're going home."

Chapter 47

The camp was alive with laughter and much cheer. Everyone was excited about going home. Captain Dillon had the officers assemble the men and he got up on a wagon and addressed them.

"Men, today we got the official word that we are going home."

There was a loud cheer.

"Before we leave, as is usual with the army, we have to account for all of our gear and assemble it, ready to be turned back to the quartermasters. So we need to clean and make ready, all guns, all wagons, all harnesses, and everything, with the exception of our uniforms and mess kits. On the last day all tents will be taken down and counted, folded and piled on wagons. Everything that belongs to the army will be given back to the army.

"We've traveled many miles and accounted for ourselves in a grand way. Let's get our unit ready and leave in the fashion that has distinguished us as one of the best."

The men cheered and it was a very happy camp that evening. We had a quite a lot of produce and a few chickens and two ducks, so we made a fine stew. We had heaping bowls of berries and someone managed to get milk and sugar for them. It was a memorable day. The camp was awake late into the night.

The next days we cleaned and counted every gun, buckle, bullet and harness. We groomed the horses and polished the guns. Everything was stacked and ready to go. Then on June 29, Captain Dillon had Preston play reveille at 3 AM. The camp woke and everyone began taking down the tents and got ready to leave. Captain Dillon called everyone into formation.

He had the unit flag brought up and had Preston play the bugle call to retire the flag. Two of the officers removed the flag from the pole and folded it. They gave it to Captain Dillon. He nodded to Foster and he began playing *The Battle Hymn of the Republic.* Everyone joined in singing. I don't think there was a dry eye in the camp.

We marched to the train station and boarded the train at 4 AM. We rode to Dechard, Tennessee and arrived there at noon. There we changed engines and all began boarding the new train. Nearly everyone was on board and the engineer threw the engine into full power and the train lurched forward violently. Men fell and there was much cursing and shouting. Then from farther back toward the end of the train there was screaming. The train was underway but soon stopped.

"What's happened?" Preston asked.

No one knew, but many left the train to see. The three of us got off and saw a group of men part way back. We walked back to see what was going on and were stopped by one of the officers.

"You don't want to see this," he said.

"What's happened?"

"One of the men fell."

"Is he hurt?"

"The train ran over him. He's had his legs cut off."

I looked at Preston and his face was as white as snow. I felt sick myself. We stood there and soon two of our men came from the front of the train with the engineer in tow. The man was staggering. He was drunk.

"Here's the drunken fool!"

When it was all over we found out it was Franklin King. He'd been on the ladder between cars when the train lurched forward and had fallen on the tracks. The train had cut off his legs. He died in minutes in the arms of his brother.

It didn't seem possible that one of our men had made it through the entire war without a scratch and then had been killed on the way home. It was a terrible tragedy.

The joy and happiness we'd all felt at going home was subdued after that.

We rode the train and stopped many times on the way home. When we finally got to Wisconsin we were all very happy. We went to Kenosha we said goodbye to Tommy since he and the men with him were taking a different train up to Green Bay. He promised to come and visit and we promised to visit him. Then we took a train to Madison where we arrived on July 18, 1865. We'd been gone three years and four months. We were mustered out of the army. The war was over.

Chapter 48

E ven though we no longer were officially in the army, we still wore our uniforms because that was all that most of us had. I was looking forward to wearing overalls and a nice cotton shirt instead of the wool uniform.

We boarded a train headed for Lone Rock.

As we headed west from Madison we looked out the windows at the hills of Wisconsin. Soon we were in the Wisconsin River valley with his high bluffs and lush green fields.

When we pulled into the train station at Lone Rock there was a huge crowd of people. They'd been told we were coming and held a homecoming for us. All of the local politicians were there and they even had a band. There were tables set up filled with food and drink. It was very exciting.

We got off the train and assembled one last time. Captain Dillon stood up on the train platform.

"Gentlemen of the Sixth Wisconsin Light Artillery. We left this place three years ago and have seen much hardship and loss but we've helped save the United States and the Union. You have done a splendid job and I thank every one of you for all your hard work and sacrifice."

He nodded to Foster and me. We began playing *Yankee Doodle*. Soon everyone was singing. When we finished, Captain Dillon saluted us.

"The Sixth Wisconsin Light Artillery is... dismissed."

There was a great shout. Men ran to their wives and families. Preston turned and his mom grabbed him and began kissing him, much to his embarrassment. Foster had his mom and dad with him hugging him. I turned and of course I had no mom or dad waiting for me.

Then I looked through the crowd and there she was. At first I wasn't sure if was her. When I left she was skinny and still just a girl. Now there was a beautiful young woman with long blond hair, sparkling blue eyes and lots of curves where women had curves. She was wearing a white blouse and blue-checkered skirt. She began running toward me with her arms wide. She ran up to me and jumped into my arms and kissed me smack dab on the mouth.

"Holy smokes Kathy Jane," I gasped.

"What's wrong Eli?"

I looked into her beautiful face, and kissed her a second time.

"Nothing's wrong Kathy Jane, not one dang thing."

The rest of the day was filled with food and drink and lots of people hugging and kissing. Kathy Jane and I held hands and walked around talking and stopping now and then for a little kiss. We came across Preston and he was with Gertie Manning. They were holding hands and giggling. Gertie had stopped wearing her hair in pigtails too but she was still a little on the husky side. Preston seemed like he had eyes only for her.

"Have you seen Foster?" I asked.

"He was talking to a bunch of girls. I didn't know any of them. I think they were from Sauk Prairie where he's from."

"That dog. He's out hunting," I said.

"Eli!" Kathy Jane said giggling.

Soon we saw Foster. He was sitting on a bench with a tall girl with dark hair and she was very well filled out. I looked at Preston and he grinned.

"You two," Gertie said.

Foster saw us and brought his new friend over.

"These are the two guys I told you about," he said. "This is Alma Daniels, she's from Sauk Prairie."

We all said hi.

"Are you old friends from before the war?" Kathy Jane asked.

"We went to school together,' Alma said, "but Foster hated girls then."

Foster blushed.

"I didn't hate them. I just didn't like them much."

"But you do now?" I asked.

He glanced at me and smirked.

"Heck yeah."

When it got dark there were fireworks and then a couple of men with fiddles and a lady with an accordion began playing music. People began dancing. The three girls tried their best to get us to dance but we wouldn't have any of it. None of us knew how.

A while later Preston and Gertie said they were going for a walk. We watched them head toward the woods. Foster and Alma left too and that left Kathy Jane and me standing there.

"Feel like walking along the river?" I asked.

She smiled and took my hand. We walked through town and down to the river. The moon shined on the water and made it look like a golden ribbon moving off into the west. We took off our shoes and walked in the wet sand.

"I've thought about being here with you for three years," I said.

She stopped and turned and we embraced and kissed.

"I never stopped thinking about you Eli."

We moved up onto the grass and sat down.

"You're so quiet Eli," she said.

I was scared to death.

"Kathy Jane, I want to ask you something."

She knew what I was going to say.

"Yes Eli."

"Yes?"

"Yes, I'm hoping you were going to ask me to be your wife."

"So you will?"

"I always knew I'd marry you someday Eli Campbell."

Wow.

I opened my eyes when I heard some kids talking. I sat up and looked around. There were two boys waking down the sand carrying fishing poles. I looked down at Kathy Jane.

"Someone's coming," I said shaking her gently.

She opened her eyes and smiled at me. Her dress was all mussed and she had sticks in her hair. My uniform shirt was all wrinkled and I had sand all over the side of my face from when I must have slept with it on the sandy ground. We quickly got ourselves together. The two kids came up to us. They looked at us like we were crazy lying on the grass by the river.

"You fishing?"

"Nope, just watching the river go by," I said.

They looked at me like I was a little crazy but then one of them got a grin on his face. He looked at Kathy Jane and then at me.

"Okay if we fish here?"

"Heck yeah," I said.

"We don't want to interrupt," the other said.

"We got to get back to town anyway," I said.

We got up and walked to town. When we got to Kathy Jane's store and house we stopped.

"Is your Ma going to have a fit?"

"She might but she'll get over it."

"Can I see you later?"

"Of course. Come back at noon and I'll bring a picnic."

I liked that idea. We had a quick kiss and she went inside. I walked down the street to the tailor shop. I really didn't have any place else to go. Captain Dillon saw me go past his house and came out. He was wearing a civilian suit with a white shirt and black tie. I hadn't seen him in anything but a uniform for so long that it took me by surprise.

"Just getting home Eli?"

I grinned. '

"Yes Sir."

"What are your plans?"

"Kathy Jane and I are going on a picnic later."

He laughed.

"I mean your plans for the future?"

I thought for a minute.

"Can you keep a secret?" I asked. He nodded. "I'm going to marry Kathy Jane and then I think I'm going to fix up my family house and do a little farming."

"That sounds like a splendid idea Eli. She's a lovely girl."

"Yes she is Sir."

"Why don't you call me Henry now? I'm not a Captain anymore."

"I couldn't do that Sir. You'll always be a Captain to me. Are you going to be a tailor again?"

"I might do a little work but I've sent my pay back all the while we've been gone, and my wife and I are buying a farm outside of town."

"I sent my pay home and Kathy Jane has been keeping it for me. Most months I sent almost all of it but a few months I spent a little for fishing hooks and stuff."

"You boys were a God-send to the unit. I can't imagine what kind of moral we'd have had without your wonderful meals."

"It was Preston that did the cooking. Foster and I peeled

stuff but he knew how to do all of that."

Captain Dillon put his hand on my shoulder. He smiled at me.

"It was a wonderful adventure wasn't it Eli?"

"Yes Sir it was, except for Bruce and Danny and the others who died."

"That's part of war Eli. We can be glad that we were privileged to know those brave men. They'll always be a part of our memory."

I nodded and felt like I was going to cry. I thought of Bruce and his silly grin and how he laughed. Next to my family no one had ever meant as much to me as he had.

"Your uniform has gotten too small for you Eli," he said.

"Yes sir. I don't have any other clothes. The ones I had before I went into the army are all too small too."

"Let's go over to the tailor shop. I have some things that will fit you."

We walked to the tailor shop. When we went inside it looked exactly like it did that last day we were there before we left for the war. The table where I sat and wrote down all the names was right where it had been and the pencil I'd used was still lying there.

Captain Dillon opened some drawers and a closet and came back with several shirts and pants and some underwear. He also had a nice suit jacket in his arms.

"These should fit you Eli.'

"I'll have to go down to the river and have a bath," I said, not wanting to put the new clothes on after not having a bath for several days.

"Come over to my house and use our tub. My wife and the kids are visiting friends."

We walked to his house and I took a bath and dressed in a new white shirt and a pair of new trousers. They actually came down to my shoes instead of half way down like my uniform did. I wrapped the uniform and my long underwear up with a piece of twine.

"I'm not going to miss those long-johns and that itchy wool uniform," I said.

"They were fine in the cool weather but it was a challenge to wear them in the summer wasn't it Eli?"

"I was proud to wear the uniform Captain."

He smiled at me.

I picked up my stuff and walked to the door. I thanked him for the clothes and for all he'd done for me.

"Any time you have a problem or need something Eli, if there's anything I can do for you, don't hesitate to ask," Captain Dillon said.

"Well there is one thing, could I borrow your buggy?"

"Of course, going on a trip?"

I grinned.

"Kathy Jane and I are going to have a picnic."

Chapter 49

I had one thing that I had to do before I went to pick up Kathy Jane. The day before I'd hoped to see Tom at the reception when we arrived but it seemed he hadn't been there. It bothered me that he wasn't there but I got caught up with... well with Kathy Jane and kind of forgot about him.

I walked down the street to his house and found him sitting in the garden down by the river. As usual he had a fishing pole leaning in a forked stick. He saw me coming and broke into a wide smile.

"Eli, my goodness, look at you all grown up."

I leaned down and put my arms around the old man and hugged him. He looked frail.

"I'm sorry I didn't get down here yesterday Tom. It was so busy with all the people and everything."

"That's fine Eli. I should have tried to get up to the celebration but sometimes it's hard to find someone to haul my old body around. Being one-legged and old, it's not easy to get places."

"How have you been? You look like you've lost weight?"

"I'm fine Eli. I had a bit of the stomach flu this spring and was off my feed. You look well. You must have grown four inches."

"You should see the others too. We're all a lot taller and pretty much grown up."

"And you all made it back with all your arms and legs and everything."

I nodded.

"You know Bruce died," I said.

He nodded and looked sad.

"He was a fine lad. I didn't know Lieutenant Noyse very well but it was sad to hear about them both, plus the other lads that died that day. It must have been a terrible battle."

"It was a day I'll never forget Tom."

"Well it's over now. What are your plans Eli?"

"I'm going to marry Kathy Jane."

His eyes lit up.

"You're going to get married?"

I nodded.

"We wrote back and forth all the while I was gone and I knew I liked her more than a friend. And then I got home and saw her."

"She's a beautiful woman Eli."

"No kidding."

"She's looked in on me many times while you were gone. I think each time you wrote she stopped and told me about your letter. I knew she was in love with you a long time ago."

"I'm going to take her to our farm today for a picnic and see what she thinks about living there. She's going to take over the store from her parents and I'm going to be a farmer."

"It sounds like you've got it all figured out Eli."

I told him about Preston and Foster and their girlfriends and he was happy for us all.

"I'm going to ask them to come and help me do some work on the farm Tom. Would you like to come out there with us and supervise?"

"I'm not much good for anything else but I'd love to come."

"I'll let you know as soon as we get it all planned. I have to go pick up Kathy Jane now."

I hugged him again.

"Thanks for visiting me Eli. You've made an old man very happy. Tell Preston and Foster hi from me too."

"I'll bring them with me next time."

I pulled the buggy into the front of Kathy Jane's house and tied the horse to a post. Her mother came out on the porch. Oh boy.

"So Elijah Campbell, you're the one who kept my daughter out all night?"

"I'm sorry ma-am. We were watching the river go by and fell asleep. I was very tired from the long trip home from fighting the war."

She looked down her nose at me.

"Well I guess that is a good reason. You'll not be out all night tonight though?"

"Oh no ma-am, we'll be back early."

"Very well."

She went in the house and Kathy Jane came out grinning. She was wearing a yellow dress and had a white ribbon in her hair tying it back. She looked beautiful and I had all I could to not to grab her and kiss her.

She was carrying a picnic basket and I took it from her and put it in the buggy. I helped her up into the seat.

"My you look handsome," she said looking me up and down.

"Thanks to Captain Dillon," I said. "I don't have any of my old clothes. They're all too small for me."

"Where shall we go for our picnic Eli?"

"I'd like to go to the farm. I haven't been there in three years."

"I'd love to see it," she said.

She put her arm through mine and I clucked at the horse and she began trotting down the road. When we were out of sight of Kathy Jane's house she leaned over and kissed me.

The sun was shining, a breeze was ruffling the leaves and I felt like the luckiest guy in the world. I'd made it through the war and had the prettiest girl in town on my arm, and she loved me. Holy smokes.

Chapter 50

Half way down the lane to the farm there was a tree lying across the road. It must have blown down in a storm. I got out and pulled on it and managed to slide it off the road far enough so we could pass.

When we pulled into the yard in front of my family house I reigned in the horse and sat looking at the place. The last time I was here I was with Bruce and I'd just buried my brother. Not much had changed. There was some junk that had blown into the yard and some branches from trees scattered around. Otherwise it looked the same.

The board that Bruce and I had nailed across the door was still there with the warning of smallpox written on it.

"Did you put that there?" Kathy Jane asked.

"Bruce and I did it. We thought that might keep someone from breaking into the house. It looks like it worked."

I jumped down from the buggy and helped Kathy Jane down. She held my hand and we walked up to the front door. I took hold of the end of the board and pulled and after a few grunts and more pulling, I got it off the door frame. I opened the door and looked inside. Everything looked exactly like it did when I was there almost four years earlier.

We walked in and stood there looking around.

"It's small but nice," Kathy Jane said.

I could tell she wasn't very impressed with it. Her house was much more grand and modern.

"I was thinking that I'd take that wall out and add some

bedrooms and make the kitchen bigger," I said.

"You can do all of that?"

"Well not by myself but if I had a little help I could. I think I've got enough money saved up to do all of that."

"You've got a lot of money Eli. I think the last time you sent me some I counted it up and there was over four-hundred dollars."

"I think I could make the place suitable for you with that much."

She looked at me and put her arms around me. She kissed me on the cheek.

"Eli I'd live in a tent if you asked me to. I've loved you since we were in fourth grade. I don't care about a fancy house as long as I have you."

We had a nice kiss. Holy smokes!

I wanted to go to where my family was buried. Kathy Jane walked part way with me and then said I should go on alone. I walked up to the little cemetery and stood there looking down at the four graves.

"I made it back from the war," I said. "I'm going to farm here and live in the house. I just wanted to let you know I'm home safe. I miss you all," I said. My chest felt tight and I had to blink a few times to keep the tears from spilling down my face.

We walked back and got the picnic basket. We walked up on the little hill behind the house and spread a blanket and sat down.

"So," I said.

"So," Kathy Jane said smiling.

"I guess I never really asked you, but will you marry me Kathy Jane?"

"Of course Eli. I knew I was going to marry you years ago. You just didn't know it yet."

"I was thinking that if you run the store, I can help when

you need me but I want to build a little barn and a chicken coop and have a little farm here. I think with both of us working, we'd be able to have a pretty good life."

"I want some babies too Eli."

Holy cow!

"Oh um, okay," I muttered.

She laughed.

"Not right this minute Eli. But when you said about building a couple of bedrooms, I was thinking maybe three or so. I grew up as an only child and I want to have a full house with lots of children, and dogs and cats and all kinds of critters."

"We've already got a dog. Preston took Crumb home for now but he's coming back with him when we start building."

"Well there you are. We have a start on a house full of love," she said.

"So when should we get married?" I asked.

"As soon as possible. I want to start working on filling those bedrooms with babies."

Chapter 51

We had our picnic and then Kathy Jane and I walked through the house and she looked it over. I could tell she was used to something nicer but she said she could see a lot of possibilities in our house. I drove the buggy down to Tom's house and found him in the garden.

"Do you know anything about building a house?" I asked.

"Are you building a house Eli?"

"Well I want to build on to my house on the farm. It's not very big and I want to add some rooms on it."

I knew I was blushing because I was thinking about Kathy Jane wanting a lot of bedrooms for a lot of babies.

"I've done some building. I wouldn't be much good for anything physical but I think I could help out with the plans and how to do things."

"I'm going to have Preston and Foster come and help me," I said.

"Well count me in."

I got word to Preston and Foster and they showed up at the farm two days later. They both brought clothes and stuff so they could stay until we were finished. Tom also came out to the farm and also planned on staying. Crumb was there too and he had a great time checking out his new home.

Tom brought a flat panel of wood and began drawing the floor plan of the old house on it. I went to town and got Kathy Jane and we sat and talked and planned while Tom drew the new blue prints.

When we were done it was a bit more than I'd planned on.

"It got a little bit bigger than I expected," I said.

"You need room for all those babies," Preston said grinning.

Oh boy, I should have never told him and Foster that. I'd never hear the end of it.

We began by tearing off part of the wall of the old house. Captain Dillon had heard of our project and drove down in the afternoon to supervise. He and Tom sat and talked while we worked.

That evening Preston made some dinner and we ate and then sat around a campfire like we'd done in the war. Tom was with us and regaled us with stories of his time in the army. It was a great night.

The next morning we had breakfast and heard the sound of someone coming down the road. We looked out and there was Captain Dillon and about half a dozen men from the unit. They were hauling equipment and had a portable sawmill on a wagon.

"Morning," Captain Dillon said.

"Good morning, what is all of this?" I asked.

"I happened to mention that you were building an addition to your house and these men volunteered to help. We brought a saw along to cut some lumber from your trees here and a shallow tub to mix cement in to make a proper foundation. Tom mentioned that he has the plans all worked out, so I'd suggest we get to work."

It was like being in the army again. Captain Dillon sent men to cut trees and drag them to the sawmill, and the others went to work framing up a foundation and began making cement in the tub. Others took a wagon and brought back big stones to add to the foundation to make it stronger. The three of us helped where we were needed and in no time we had a heck of a good start on the house.

"I figured we'd be here all summer," Preston said as he and I stood looking over the finished foundation walls.

"No kidding. I didn't even know that we needed a foundation," I said.

He laughed.

"It's a good thing they showed up. We'd have built you a house and it would have fallen down with all your babies inside it."

I punched him in the arm.

We worked for the next five weeks and at the end of that last week, the house was finished. Each day more men came to work and then one day, Preston's girlfriend Gertie and Foster's girlfriend Alma showed up with Kathy Jane and they began working inside, painting and finishing things up. We had a big party and feast when it was all done.

Captain Dillon came over by me as the party wound down.

"Well Eli, I think you have a fine home here now."

"Thanks to you Sir. Preston and Foster and I would still be trying to figure out how to build that first wall. I'll never be able to repay you and all of the men."

"They were glad to help. We went through a war together and will remain friends and brothers forever."

Preston and Foster and their girlfriends stayed with us. They helped me build a small barn and a chicken coop and a horse shelter for Franklin. The girls went to Madison on the train and came back with things for the house two days later. I didn't want to ask how much money I had left.

We were eating dinner that night and Preston announced that he and Gertie were going to buy the diner in town. The people who owned it were retiring and they had worked out to buy it from them. They were going to live next door in a little house that the owners had live in.

Foster had been talking to Captain Dillon and he was going to train him to do tailoring. He was going to rent the tailor shop and give it a try. Kathy Jane had already found that she needed help running the store and she had talked to Alma about working there.

"So all of us have girlfriends who will soon be wives and we all have plans for the future," I said.

"We've come a long way from three kids playing a bugle, fife and drums," Preston said.

"We sure have."

Chapter 52

L ife was good. Our house was perfect, we had our best friends close by and our future looked great. It was quite a change from a few years earlier as I watched my whole family die of small pox and was left alone.

The weather was turning cooler and Preston, Foster and I were going to do some squirrel hunting. After a few hours of hunting we stopped for a drink of spring water from a spring coming out of the hillside.

"You know, today is the anniversary of the day at Corinth," Preston said.

"Really?"

"It's October 4th. It was three years ago today," he said.

"We should go and visit Bruce's grave," I said.

They both nodded.

We drove the wagon down the road and stopped at Button Cemetery. The leaves had already started falling and the ground was scattered with them. We spread out and looked around and soon I found his grave. I called the guys over.

We stood there looking at the stone. It had his real first name, Leonidas on it.

"Bruce was just as brave, as that King Leonidas," Foster said.

"That he was. Maybe too brave," I said.

We stood there looking at his gravestone. At the bottom was carved, 20 years, 28 days.

"He was too young to die," I said.

"There were many who were too young," Preston said.

Over the next few months, all of us got married. Kathy Jane and I had our wedding later that autumn. Since I didn't have any kinfolk to stand up with me, I asked Captain Dillon to be my best man and of course Preston and Foster were my groomsmen. After the wedding we moved into our remodeled house and spent a very exciting winter.

Preston was next and got married in the spring followed two weeks later by Foster. Now we all had wives and felt pretty grown up. I really felt grown up later that summer when Kathy Jane delivered our first baby.

It was a little boy and we named him Bruce. There was no doubt about that.

Over the next few years my two best friends and I filled our homes with babies. Mine were all boys, at least so far. After Bruce came Danny and without a doubt, the next one was Henry. Kathy is pregnant again and she is hopeful she'll have at least one girl.

Preston and Foster also have several kids each. Some day when they all start going to school, it will get a little confusing. They each named their first son Bruce.

Henry Ashby came back to Wisconsin with us and spent some time in Lone Rock. Then one day he stopped by and told me he was leaving for Eagle River.

"Eagle River? Why there?" I asked.

"Doesn't it sound like a wonderful place?"

I had to admit it sounded pretty nice compared to a place like Lone Rock.

I shook hands with him.

"It's been an honor to know you Henry," I said.

"The honor was all mine Eli. You and your friends treated me better than I'd ever been treated before. I'll always remember you kindly."

Chapter 53

The Sixth Wisconsin Light Artillery reported to Camp Utley, Racine in September 1861. We had signed up 157 men and when we got to Racine we gained eighty-two recruits, two substitutes and thirty-four reenlistments. Our total unit consisted of two hundred and seventy five men. We lost twenty-nine men during our time at war. One was our dear friend Lieutenant Danny Noyse and of course one of my best friends, Bruce Honn. We lost five men at Corinth. The rest of the men who died from the Sixth did so of disease or of infection from wounds. Two were taken prisoner and thirty-six were disabled. We had five deserters and seven were discharged for one thing or another. We mustered out one hundred and ninety six men.

Thomas Hood, our other Captain mustered out with the rest of us on July 3, 1865. He died less than two years later after being kicked in the head by a horse. He came through the war without a scratch and lost his life in such a simple accident. He was thirty-one years old.

Lieutenant Alba Sweet also died just a few weeks after Captain Hood in a tragic accident. He was helping his brother Nicholas Sweet, also a member of the 6th to raise timbers for his new house. A log rolled and knocked him thirteen feet to the ground and then struck him as he fell.

Captain Dillon had sent his pay home all the while he was at war and when he got home he and his wife purchased a farm outside of Lone Rock. There was a small cabin on the farm and they moved a house from Lone Rock to the place and connected them. He farmed and was active in politics and kept very busy.

He had twelve children during his life and several died quite young. His first son Freddie had died as a baby in 1858 and then another baby daughter Katie was born and died in 1867. Six-year old Hattie died in 1868 and his oldest daughter Susan died in 1880.

The greatest tragedy occurred in 1882 when he went to care for a neighboring family who was suffering from smallpox. He'd always thought that he was immune but it wasn't so. He contracted smallpox and unknowingly brought the disease home to his family. The Captain, his son Bruce and a daughter all died. He'd survived two wars, led men into battle and come home only to lose his life by being kind to another. His loss was a blow to all who knew him and respected him.

Chapter 54

Standing at the grave of the man I most respected in my life I had a hard time keeping the tears back. When I was a boy with no one in the world, Henry Dillon befriended me and helped me out. When it turned out I was too young to join the unit, he found a way for me to go and be a part of the great adventure. When we got home he looked in on me and was always there for me.

I stood there and looked up at my beautiful wife and my three sons standing in their Sunday best and vowed that I'd try to be a man like him. There were many brave men and boys who set off to war, but there was only one Captain Henry Dillon who led them and brought most of them home. He'd led an amazing life and had died as he lived, helping others.

I still go to the Button Cemetery often. I can see Bruce with a goofy grin on his face, laughing at some prank he pulled on one of us. I can hear his voice and his laugh. I often wonder what he'd have done in his life had he come home with us. He'll be forever young.

And I stand by Captain Dillon's grave and remember his big voice and stern attitude. But it was all a show. Underneath he was the nicest man I'd ever met.

Preston, Foster and I set off as three boys, who wanted to be a part of something that would change us forever. We had no idea what we were getting into but we made it through and learned a lot about ourselves and other people. We learned that people are the same north or south. We talk a little differently and have a few different customs, but we're all the same, black or white, north or south.

I think the war was worth fighting. It wasn't right for people to own other people. There were over a million casualties in the Civil War. Over six hundred thousand people died during the war. Many more were disabled and crippled for life. But it had to be done to keep the United States together.

I saw more of the country than I ever expected to see. Had it not been for the Civil War, I'd probably have never left the Wisconsin River valley. But I left and when I got home I figured something out. This country is vast and beautiful but there's no place like this river valley. I'll be content to live here in this beautiful place with my wife and children and my friends who I went to war with, until I join the friends I lost someday... and then we'll have a grand reunion.

ABOUT THE AUTHOR

Dan Bomkamp has made his home in the Wisconsin River valley all his life with the exception of his college years in La Crosse. He has been an avid hunter and fisherman his whole life. For many years he was in the sporting goods industry and began writing in the 80s for outdoor magazines. He is active in the Foreign Exchange Student program having hosted 33 boys from 13 countries over the years. Golden Retrievers have also been a big part of his life. He had at least one Golden sharing his home for 33 years. He lives in Muscoda with his cat, Tigger and his Boston Terrier, Buster.

E-mail: Danbomkamp@live.com
Website: www.Danbomkamp.com

Other books by Dan Bomkamp

The Adventures of Thunderfoot
More Adventures of Thunderfoot
Thanks, Thunderfoot
The Gosey
Big Edna
Voyageur
Lost Flight
Tag
Whiteout
Spirit
The Lost Treasure of Bogus Bluff
November Gales
Bringing Ethan Home
The Boy Who Fell From the Sky

Non-Fiction
River of Mystery

Made in the USA
Middletown, DE
28 September 2020

20667674R00126